# RESURGENCE

## DOGS OF WAR
## BOOK 5

## JM MADDEN

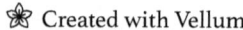

Thank you beta readers for always putting up with my bad timing! LOL

Sandie, Deb, Belinda, Eve and Karen- you guys rock! Thank you for the input!

# 1

One minute he was kicking ass like the Army Ranger he used to be, the next he was on the practice mat, trying to regain the breath that had been knocked out of him.

Haven Wendell blinked up at the fluorescent lights, a little shocked at how quickly the world had spun out of control. Then he grinned up at Copper and took his proffered hand. "No fair, big man. I'm still recovering from driving from Colorado yesterday."

Copper snorted as he righted him. "Right. Like you didn't just sleep for twelve hours."

Haven grimaced. "I did not sleep that long. Maybe ten," he murmured, grinning, as he knocked into Copper's shoulder. "It was damn good sleep, too."

The week in Denver had been a little crazy. Aiden and Angela had wanted to introduce Baby Fallon to the Lost and Found crew, so they'd flown out for the company Christmas party. Unfortunately, they'd been attacked, and baby Fallon had almost been taken. The men who attacked them were in the custody of the CIA, but Haven thought someone else had been out there as well, running the show behind the scenes. It all went back to former senator Cameron Hall. He was in prison, now, but Haven and the rest of the Dogs of War felt like he was still pulling the strings and trying to reacquire Belladonna.

As if thinking about her made her materialize, Donna Frame stepped into the gym, dressed in sweats and a gray ARMY T-shirt, as well as running shoes. Her long dark hair was drawn back into a French-braid, then bunned low on her head. It was how she normally dressed when she came down for training or even just working out, and Haven was suddenly uncomfortable with how happy it made him to see her. His gaze soaked her in. He'd only been away from the Elton building for a five days, but it had seemed longer. Her dark eyes flashed up to his, and he wondered if she'd gotten some indication of what he was thinking. She gave him a slight, polite smile, then headed for the bench on the far side of the room. She dropped a towel there, and a bottle of water, then climbed on the treadmill.

Damn it. That polite smile meant she'd probably heard something from him, because he certainly hadn't been thinking about shielding his mind as she'd walked in.

"Guess you're done training with me," Copper murmured, snorting softly.

Haven flashed him an apologetic look.

"Sorry, big man. She's a hell of a lot prettier than you are."

Copper flashed an aggrieved face.

"Seriously? I combed my hair just for you," he said, running his fingers through his thick auburn hair.

Haven grinned, shaking his head. "Go show the rest of the guys how pretty you are."

With an exaggerated harrumph, Copper turned toward the group at the weight rack.

Haven sighed, wondering if he should turn around and go

shower or go see her. Who was he kidding? He knew he was going to go over and see her. Wiping his face on his t-shirt, he headed across the room toward the line of treadmills.

"You're back," Donna said, glancing at him. "And safely. I was worried."

Donna was a woman of few words, and that was almost relief he heard in her voice. Had she been worried about him? "Think I wasn't coming back?"

Rather than answer him, she turned back to the digital readout of the treadmill, bumping the speed up a little. She went from a slow walk to a faster walk, warming up. Haven climbed onto the treadmill beside her, and matched her speed. They walked companionably for a few minutes before she bumped it up to a jog. He paced her. For shits and giggles, he created a dog to run beside them on the next treadmill. The treadmill wasn't on, of course, and the dog wasn't real, but it was a challenge to make it *look* real. To make the mechanics work correctly. He shaped the animal into a long-haired German Shepherd. With big teeth.

When he'd been released from the torture camp in Guyana, it had taken him a long time to realize that he was no longer being tortured. His brain had created an elaborate oubliette in his mind, and the ayahuasca serum Dr. Shu had pumped into his body had given him the ability to manifest protectors. They had no physical mass, but he'd gotten good enough now that even close up they looked as real as the flesh and blood soldiers, or real fire. Back then, the apparitions were enough to spook the superstitious, native guards, and he'd earned himself a place at the edge of camp, barely cared for. That had been to his detriment, obviously, but by that point, he was ready to give up. He'd been in the torture camp for months, receiving injection after injection. Some were meant to make him stronger- the ayahuasca concoctions they called Spartan meant to genetically engineer his DNA.

And others were meant to destroy him. He knew for a fact he'd gotten Denguay fever and hepatitis, as well as several variations of anthrax and typhoid. Spartan had cured them all, though, as far as he could tell. Dr. Elizabeth Cole, Wulfe's wife, took blood samples every month, and he'd been clear ever since he'd been rescued by the Dogs of War from the Guyana camp.

At the time he'd been rescued, he'd been on the verge of death. He was very thankful the team had spotted him and liberated him from that hellhole.

That was where he'd first seen Belladonna. She had been complicit with Dr. Shu's program, they'd thought. It was only last year that they'd discovered she had been as much of a prisoner as they had been. Damon Wilkes, Dr. Cole's former husband, had stolen Belladonna's daughter Lilly away to force her to comply with Dr. Shu's demands, and it had been perfect leverage. Donna had been forced to do the man's bidding, and Haven had a feeling she'd only told them a portion of what she'd had to do to survive.

Haven was struggling with an uncomfortable fondness for the woman. She'd been through so much, and she had changed her life completely since she'd been liberated. And it was visible in her beautiful face. She'd gained a little weight, and the dark circles weren't as pronounced as they'd once been.

Donna wasn't a woman who used her looks to her advantage, though she could. The dark eyes and hair hinted at a Hispanic heritage somewhere, but she was tall. He was a hair over six feet, and she was just a few inches shorter. It was her demeanor that appealed to him, though. The woman was unflappable. Calm and exceptionally cool, her pale face showed little emotion, her eyes steady. He knew part of that was from her military career, but even more so, it was from everyone looking at her like she was a pariah. Donna had perfected 'resting bitch face', though he knew for a fact she was anything but. It was all a mask, that the men were slowly beginning to see. He had seen her kindness, and her warmth. And he had tasted it upon his lips.

But that had been more than a year ago. Since then, she'd kept him at arm's length.

*They're circling, looking for a weakness.*

Haven wasn't surprised she spoke to him telepathically. It was her preferred method when there was the slightest possibility they could be overheard. Knowing that there were men in the world like Noah Cross, who could hear a car door slam two miles away, made one leery of speaking out loud. They had no idea how many men had been treated with Shu's drugs, let alone the abilities those drugs gave the men.

*I know,* he returned. *You heard about Denver, then.*

*I did. They're getting more desperate.*

Yeah, that's what he was thinking too. *Fallon definitely has something going on. I can get impressions from her, anger, fear. I shouldn't be able to get anything from her.*

Donna glanced at him slightly, her dark brows raised. *You know who her father is.*

Haven smiled slightly, bowing his head. Aiden had one of the strongest minds Haven had ever experienced. *I do, but I don't think anyone expected her to be this active this early.*

*No,* she agreed. *But then, as far as we know, no other babies have been born yet with the modified DNA in their bloodstream.*

*True.*

*When Shu was alive, he thought the second generation, meaning the offspring from the soldiers, would be more refined. If the abilities carried over. He had no idea if they would or not. He talked about creating a home for the babies the soldiers produced.*

Haven winced, truly hoping no such place existed. He couldn't imagine a baby or child being subjected to Shu's tender loving care. Luckily, a viper, of all things, had taken the crazed doctor out in the jungles of Brazil, and they didn't have to worry about that.

Haven settled into the rhythm of the jog, matching her stride for stride, and wondered what other surprises they were going to have to deal with. Dr. Shu had been a genius, modifying the hallucinogenic properties in the ayahuasca plant to enhance latent mental abilities. Soldiers had been ideal test subjects, because very often they had enhanced senses already, as well as strict control. The drugs highlighted those abilities and basically put them into overdrive. Dr. Elizabeth Cole, Wulfe's wife, was studying the repercussions of the drug on the men they'd rescued, because it was still changing them, now on a molecular level. And there was no method to the madness. There was no predicting what the enhanced ability would be. It was like a huge roulette wheel of abilities had been doled out. Enhanced hearing, telepathic abilities, echo-location, flora manipulation. They even had one man who had a strong connection to animals, and another who could manipulate water. Fontana had an affinity to electricity. Elizabeth was trying to see if the powers manifested correlated to the torture they'd gone through, but so far, every ability seemed random.

And they were still having casualties. They'd rescued half a dozen men from a Mexican camp just a couple of months ago, and they were all struggling down on the second floor. One of the men had died a couple of times, but Dr. Cole had been able to bring him back. Baron's skin sloughed off each time he died, like a lizard. Haven wouldn't have believed it if he hadn't seen it himself.

Haven thought there was someone, or a group of some-ones, out there continuing the tests. There had to be. The possibilities of having an enhanced army would be worth any amount of money and risk. If their group was still finding survivors, some other group was still testing. They just weren't sure who it could be. Senator Cameron Hall was in prison now under a long list of criminal charges. He'd been Damon Wilkes' number one supporter, and he'd seen the possibilities of enhanced soldiers for the United States military. The man had gone overboard, though. Haven doubted he would ever see the light of day. At least, officially. The former senator still had strong friends, though, men who had supported him through the trial and beyond. It appeared that someone, or a group of someones, had taken over the reins of Hall's enterprise.

"Any word on the property in North Carolina?"

Donna blinked her dark eyes at the change of subject. "Nothing in the past few days. It's coming along nicely, Dr. Cole says. Jordyn and Fontana have been down there a few weeks now, and they seem to be progressing, in spite of the cold and snow."

Damn. He was a little jealous of that. The thought of getting back into the woods, with no one around for miles was so appealing. It had been his favorite part of being an Army Ranger. Being outside with the elements, even if they were harsh.

Donna was eyeing him, her dark brows lowered as her arms pumped. *You like the outside.*

*Of course. It's where I was trained and it's where I grew up. I was always an outside kid.*

*And where was that?*

*Where did I grow up? Rural Alabama. My family has been farming for five generations. Corn and cattle, mostly. Some cotton and peanuts for variety.*

Donna's brows lifted. She hadn't envisioned him as a farmer, obviously. He grinned at her. "What, you can't see it?"

She shook her head slowly, a slight smile curling the edges of her mouth. "I think, when everything is an emergency, you forget that people have lives and histories. Childhoods."

Haven looked forward, waving a hand slightly. It was easy to remember the old sycamore tree he'd hung out under with his brother for so many years. And the old black and white border collie that went everywhere with them, with the odd three-legged gait. He brought up a picture of his dad on the old John Deere, straw hat shading his face from the Alabama sun. It had been merciless at times, burning the fields of crops to nothing some years. As the memory flashed through his mind, he let Donna it see on the wall in front of him. He also kept a thread of attention going to the running German Shepherd. His ability had expanded tremendously in the past year, and trying to keep two strong apparitions going while he physically exerted himself was a hell of a challenge.

*Where is your mother?*

Haven frowned, the scene changing. His mother had had dark hair like him, but her eyes had been lighter, maybe blue? He remembered her standing at the stove a lot, a stained dishtowel over her shoulder as she cooked. The scene changed to her bending down in front of him, and buttoning his shirt before they went to church, then combing her fingers through his hair. The scene faded away, and he focused on his footfalls.

*I don't remember her much. She died when I was ten. From plain old pneumonia.*

*I'm sorry, Haven. I think you looked like her, with your dark hair and the set of your eyes. The color must be from your father, though.*

He flashed her a smile. *Yeah. Muddy brown.*

*Or warm, melted chocolate.*

Haven wasn't sure if he was supposed to hear that last bit, or not.

They jogged for a few minutes.

*I liked seeing your farm, and the outside. I miss it,* she admitted.

*Yeah, I get that.*

Donna and her daughter were high-risk targets, and they were inside the building twenty-four seven. Haven felt bad, because at least they could go out on ops. Hell, he could drive down the street for takeout if he wanted to. The two women couldn't.

Donna's pace began to slow, and she settled to a walk. A frown had settled onto her face, and Haven felt bad for reminding her how locked down they were. Glancing to the right, he let the apparition of the dog go. It had been pretty good, and he'd maintained it their entire jog. He could feel the tiredness from the expenditure, though. Using mental abilities taxed you just as much, if not more, than physical exertion.

There was a bench against the outer wall. She settled onto it and took a big drink from her water bottle.

"I'm sorry you can't go out," he said, settling down beside her.

She shook her head. "It's not that. Not really."

Grabbing a towel from the back of the bench, she wiped her damp face, then her neck. Haven took a swig from his own water bottle.

*I just... feel like it's never going to end. We're always getting ready for the next emergency. Or dealing with the repercussions from the last emergency.*

*You're not in an emergency right now.*

*No, but it feels like I'm going to be soon.*

Haven scanned her face. She did look tense, like she was about to be hit with something.

*Have you talked to the counselor recently?*

She shook her head. *I want no part of that man. He gives me the creeps.*

*Why?*

*I'm not sure. I scanned him but there was nothing obvious. I just don't trust him.*

*Did you tell Dr. Cole?*

*No, she has enough to worry about besides my neuroses.*

Haven was worried now. Belladonna had had a horrific time serving the senator, and he didn't think she had recovered from it. The signs of post traumatic stress were there. He moved closer to her and leaned down to get a better look at her face. Daring to reach out, he clasped her hand in his own. *Donna, you need to realize that you can't save us all. We have security all around this building, inside and out. There are at least four men on every floor. You have to be assured that they can do their job. In this moment, you are safe.*

She blinked, then her eyes softened as she looked at him. "I know, Haven. I do. But there's this bubble of anxiety that just sits in my gut. Hall is still pulling strings, and I think one of his friends has taken over operations. I think they're still making enhanced soldiers somewhere, and now that I'm not weeding out the truly dangerous ones, I'm afraid of what is going to happen. Rogue soldiers may start popping up anywhere, and we're responsible. If not directly, at least indirectly."

Haven frowned. "We can't be responsible for other's actions. We're doing our best to find these men and ease them into a maintenance program, but we can't be responsible for everything that happens in relation to this drug. There's no way."

She frowned, but didn't say anything further.

"And how is Lilly doing with being secluded? She seems to enjoy the training."

For the first time, her expression lifted. "She's doing wonderfully. Better than I expected. She gripes about not being able to go out, but I think she'll be okay. She griped about the training, too, but more than once she's reminded me to get moving for it."

As soon as Haven had recovered enough himself, he'd implemented some basic self-defense coursework for the women. The New York incident had been eye-opening for everyone, and they'd all realized they needed to be more able to protect themselves, be it nurse or former Army soldier. Nurse Raine came to the class, Donna, Lilly, even Dr. Cole had joined them several times. It was good physical exertion and it could save their lives. Over the months more of the women had joined them, and it was usually a full class three nights a week. They'd progressed on from basic self-defense to actual combat, and Haven was impressed with the women's abilities. Haven had recruited his fire team to help with the training.

"I see her in the greenhouse a lot."

In an effort to get some greenery into their life, Dr. Cole had installed a rooftop greenhouse on top of the building. It was one of the few areas of the building that didn't feel like a hospital or jail, and the residents were encouraged to go there as much as possible. It was still cold, even in Virginia, but the enclosed greenhouse took up almost the entire rooftop space. There were benches and small bistro tables scattered inside, so that people could stop and linger, enjoying the fresh scents. There were flowers blooming even now, and Haven wondered if it wasn't because Evan Spence spent so much time up there. He had a natural affinity for any growing thing, and the greenhouse was in danger of collapsing because it was so full.

Donna nodded, smiling slightly. "It seems to feed her soul. Even though she was technically a captive in New York, she had a few friends up there from school. She's missing them and she snaps out, sometimes."

"So, you get the brunt of it," he murmured.

She shrugged, lightly. "A bit. But I have her with me."

Her other hand drifted up to her neck, and Haven knew she was thinking about the collar she'd worn with the potassium chloride cocktail inside it. Her life had literally been a button push away from death. There was still a scarred area on her fair skin where the needles rode, and a ring of discoloration around her neck, and he wondered if it would ever completely fade. Very often she wore scarves around her neck. He knew she felt self-conscious.

"Is there anything I can do for the two of you?"

Donna shook her head and gave him a smile, squeezing his hand. "No, you've done more than enough for us, Haven."

Haven lived for her smiles, and her direct looks. The woman was beautiful, but she'd been beaten down by life. And circumstances. Haven would love to whisk her away to some tropical island and make her genuinely laugh, but that would be impossible right now. They had to make do with where they were in life, and there was too much danger to them all to go jaunting off.

Before he could think better of it, he raised her hand to his lips. It was just a light kiss, but it was the most they'd done since they'd been here. When she'd been trying to escape she'd kissed him, but it had been to *finesse* information into him. He remembered the feel of her lips on his own, though. After he'd gotten over the fear she was about to kill him, he'd enjoyed the kiss. It was obvious that she hadn't kissed him for pleasure. She'd been packing info into his brain so that he could get out and get help.

It had worked, of course, because everything she did worked. He didn't even remember walking to the CIA safe house, just that he knew the directions. How had she known about the safe house? He had no idea.

Donna's mind was a wonder. Haven had seen her do things so effortlessly, and casually. Things that had taken him months to master. Dr. Cole hadn't said outright, but he knew she wanted to study Donna, in depth, if just because of the healing ability she had. Dr. Cole knew not to scare her, though.

When Donna's fingers tightened on his, he took it for the acknowledgement it was and stood. Donna was one of those people that were naturally reserved, and with what had been done to her, Haven was pleased that she'd even accepted his hand. Donna had gone out of her way not to touch him, unless it was during a healing, or sometimes during class.

"I'm going to go grab a Coke and a shower," he said, pushing to his feet. "And maybe another nap."

"You know that caffeine will keep you awake," she murmured, one side of her mouth tipping up slightly.

Haven grinned and shrugged. "With the way I'm feeling right now, nothing will keep me awake. I'm bone tired. And I need to be sharp tomorrow."

Donna nodded, her eyes drifting sightlessly into the middle distance. "I understand. I feel something building, Haven, and I'm not sure how to protect from it."

"We'll just do what we always do, and roll with the punches."

DONNA WATCHED HAVEN WALK AWAY, and really tried not to be distracted by the way his hips moved in the sweats. She dragged her gaze away, shaking her head at herself. She'd been in this damned building for too long. Stared at the walls too long. Maybe she was finally falling off her rocker.

No, she knew that wasn't it. Haven was a nice guy, and he was just trying to be nice to her. That was why he worked out with her all the time. The other men didn't, if they didn't have to. There was still too much history between she and the men for it to be swept under the rug. Even now, she could feel the stares from around the room. They were waiting for her to show her 'true' colors and go off on them, or something.

For a moment, tiredness overwhelmed her, and it wasn't because of the jog. She was tired of being the strong one. Tired of always taking the high road when she overheard the men's public thoughts and didn't react to them. Tired of trying to prove she wasn't the monster Cameron Hall and Dr. Shu had made her.

The only person she didn't have to prove herself to was Haven. In spite of her history, he'd been like a rock. She didn't let him in often, because she worried that he was a little swayed by what she'd done for him. But he'd been such a staunch supporter over the past year. And those eyes of his... he'd been in the military all of his professional life. His body was strong and lean from working out and training, but he had the most kind, intelligent brown eyes. They drew her in and tempered the wild emotion she fought to keep under control.

Wiping her face with the towel one more time, she headed for the door out of the workout room, dispelling the image. Maybe by the time she got up to their apartment, Lilly would be done with her virtual learning class and they could play a game or something. She needed a distraction.

# 2

Roger McCullough stretched his neck and sighed, leaning heavily against the brick wall. This was not going to go well. He punched the icon on the burner phone.

Nicholas Pike answered on the first ring. "Update me."

McCullough went over what they'd done in Colorado and the trip back. "I can't get near the baby. She's too closely guarded."

"Well, obviously," the man said, voice snide. "I told you that before you traipsed out there."

McCullough didn't say anything, though he wanted to reach through the phone line and strangle the little asshole. He couldn't stand the guy. He was senior to Pike by about five years, but the kid had the senator's ear, and his wallet. If McCullough wanted anything, he had to go through Pike. And while the senator was locked up, he was the one bankrolling everything.

"We need to get Belladonna back," Pike said. "She's the primary. Have you seen her?"

"No, we haven't. She has to be in the building, but we haven't seen her or the girl."

"Something needs to change," Pike said, and McCullough could hear the clink of ice on glass. The punk kid was obviously making himself at home in the senator's vacant New York condo. "The experiments we're conducting with the new recruits are all failing. We need her to sort through the men to tell us which ones are viable. We're putting down more than can be used."

McCullough gritted his teeth at the information. He didn't know how he did it, but Pike was finding more recruits. More servicemen were dying, even as they thought they were supporting the country. "The drug is wrong, not the men," he growled, but Pike never listened to him.

The situation was untenable, and once again, he thought about disappearing. Just walking away. Oh, if he only could. The senator had dragged him into a hell of a mess. There was a bounty on his head, and he doubted he could walk into any bus station or airport without his face setting off every alarm. He was tired of living out of a duffle bag and eating cheap takeout.

"I need money," McCullough told him.

Pike snorted. "Oh, I'm sure you do. Seems like all I do is give you money."

McCullough nearly snarled. "You need to try living on the run on cash, with no cards. It's not easy."

"Hmm. I'll send it to the Western Union we used before."

Of course he would. Because he didn't think about the security ramifications of being in the same place more than once. Where cameras recorded every second of every day.

McCullough had given up trying to explain being on the run to the punk. It seemed to go in one ear and out the other.

"I need results, McCullough. We have to get her back."

"I'm doing what I can," he said, teeth clenched. "I'll call you when I have something."

"You'd-"

McCullough took way too much satisfaction in hanging up on the kid's empty threats. He was a former Marine, and a former Secret Service agent. The kid in charge was a damn intern. A nobody. But he was the senator's lackey, and he did what the man said. Every single time.

Somehow, Nicholas Pike was the last face in the senator's entourage. The rest of the staff had been charged with conspiracy, obstruction of justice and perjury. Most of them had been convicted, and several of his closest staff were in prison with him, at a swanky minimum security prison in West Virginia. The senator himself had taken a plea deal and managed to get out of a lot of the charges against him. He still had friends in high places, and it was obviously working for him. More than once, he'd bragged that the sitting president was one of his best friends. As soon as the shit hit the fan, though, President Kelvin disavowed knowledge of Senator Hill's transgressions. McCullough knew for a fact that the president still had two guards that were enhanced with Spartan.

Former senator Hall had a hard-on for Belladonna. She'd testified against him in a series of private depositions, and had single-handedly put him away. McCullough had a feeling Hall would enjoy using her for a while, then destroying her.

Shaking his head, he pushed away from the wall and headed for the Wal-mart thirty miles away.

WULFE SCOWLED as he listened to Aiden's report.

"So, your child is definitely a target."

Aiden nodded, mouth tight. "It seems so. Angela is upset."

"Of course she is. She is a mama tiger."

Aiden smiled slightly. Yes, that was apt.

"How is The Reserve coming?"

Wulfe rocked back in his office chair. "Good, I think. I don't hear much out of Fontana, so I have to assume it's going to plan. He'll let us know if there are issues."

Yes, he would. Or Jordyn, the more level-headed of the couple, would.

It had occurred to the Dogs months ago that they would need a second location for training and just for living. They also knew, though, that most of the men in the building would not want to interact with the general public on a daily basis. Or even a weekly basis. There were men in the building who would live on a deserted island if they were given a choice.

The three original couples, Wulfe and Elizabeth, Aiden and Angela, and Fontana and Jordyn, had gotten together and brainstormed a secondary location. They'd found a mountain range parcel in northwestern North Carolina that was fairly uninhabited. It was the tallest range east of the Mississippi, and adjoined the Mount Mitchell state park. The property consisted of over five thousand acres of almost-untouched land; two mountain peaks, as well as several adjoining smaller hills. There was a river at the base of one mountain, and several melt streams. They would have running water, even at the topmost peak. It would take a lot of work to make it habitable and safe, but it would be an amazing training ground and escape from the real world.

Aiden was excited to see the property, but he understood that there had to be a division of work. As soon as Fontana gave the go-ahead, he wanted to go down. It excited him, the thought of getting back into the woods, even in the depths of winter. And if Fontana secured the property like they wanted,

Aiden had a feeling it would be more secure than anything they could do in the city.

They had plans to make the central portion of the property the most secure, with a ten-foot fence and razor-wire. They wanted to call it The Reserve. The name also gave the connotation of a game reserve, which would explain to the locals what the men were doing up on the property. Elizabeth had hired a crew to come in known for building tree houses. They would teach the team Fontana had taken, and by the time they were done, there would be a village of tree houses swaying in the canopy, in addition to regular cabins. There would also be a central lodge built in the cleavage of the two mountains, with the ice melt stream flowing beneath it. The main lodge would be huge, and it would be the base of operations for the reserve. There would also be a hospital area, in case some of the men needed to get out sooner.

Aiden had a feeling it would be months before the lodge was ready, but two of the treehouses were almost finished, as well as three cabins. The group had been down there almost four months, roughing it in the cold as they settled in. Aiden didn't relish them that aspect, per se, but he would tolerate it if it meant having a new place to retreat to.

They had spoken to a bunch of the Elton Building residents about The Reserve, and they were careful to lay out that no one would be required to stay there. The fence would be to keep curious people and random hikers from Mount Mitchell park out. Not to keep the residents in. The residents understood and seemed as excited as Fontana had been when he'd seen the property.

The Elton building would still remain their primary location, used to treat the more severe medical cases. And it would be the base of operations for the Task Force Omega group when they were in service. When they were out of service they would have the option to head to the Reserve.

They would probably have to hire a second helicopter pilot, in addition to Jordyn, to ferry the men back and forth.

The undertaking was massive, and Aiden knew it had cost Elizabeth an even more massive amount of money. But she didn't even flinch at the projected cost. Actually, Aiden thought that she might be excited for the Reserve as well. Later, once it was more habitable. For now she would stay in the city with the amenities she enjoyed.

And for now, they were keeping the Reserve on a need-to-know basis. The CIA didn't need to know, or anyone else they'd worked for recently. They'd told General Holtman, but they knew he would keep the information under his hat. The General enjoyed having little tidbits of information that others didn't.

"So, what do we do to secure Fallon?" Wulfe asked.

Aiden sighed, rubbing a hand over his face. He'd slept through the night for the first time in a week, but he still felt jet-lagged. "I'm not even sure. Have someone with her twenty-four seven. Tag her sleepers with GPS trackers."

Wulfe lifted a dark brow at him, and Aiden laughed. "Believe me, we've thought about this. We've also thought about just disappearing. Packing everything up, getting new identities and disappearing into obscurity."

"Do you think that would work?" Wulfe asked him, and Aiden could hear the humor in the other man's voice.

"No," he sighed. "But Elton isn't one hundred percent safe either."

"Here we have the back-up we need if something goes wrong. We have the general on speed-dial, as well as Officer Rose. And most of the time one of the Delta teams are in residence. "

Aiden nodded, though he still wasn't settled. Haven had voiced just last night, as they pulled into the building, what Aiden had been thinking.

They were being stalked, and he was tired of being the mouse.

~

LILLY DANCED a finger over the dark petals of the black 'witchcraft' orchid, amazed that it could grow in the midst of winter. It was her favorite in the greenhouse, and she watched every day for signs that it was about to lose its petals. For the past month, it had appeared healthy. The stems were strong and the blooms full and richly colored, sprouting from the large clay pot they were in.

Lilly loved the plant. There were other orchids around the space, but this one captured her imagination. Who had created it? Or was it one of the naturally occurring plants? She had no idea. She doubted the dirt man would tell her.

She felt a little guilty calling the guy that, but it suited him. Though he had to be younger than her mom and Haven, he appeared older because of what he did out here. Every time she saw him, he was carrying a bucket of dirt with him to some other location. Or a plant. It seemed like busy-work to her, but what did she know? She was just a kid.

Even if she did ask Evan a question, she doubted he would answer her. The man ignored her completely. Lilly was used to being unseen, but he took it to a new level. Her mother had tried to explain to her that Evan was recovering, but he seemed fine. And he looked fine, she thought with a slight flush. But her mother obviously didn't think he was a danger if she allowed Lilly to be up here with him.

Lilly tapped the screen of her laptop and logged into Wattpad. She had two stories she was following, and they each were supposed to post today. She wished she had her phone, but that had been taken when she'd been rescued from the senator's house. He had supplied it, so she kind of understood, but man she missed talking to her friends. And reading everywhere she went. Having to lug the laptop around was a pain in the ass.

It was almost an hour later when something made her look up. The sun was going down outside the greenhouse, but it was still light enough to see. A chill rolled over her skin, and she began packing up her things. She hadn't seen the silent Evan for a while, so maybe it was time to go in. Maybe he already had, just leaving her out here, all alone.

The thought should have made her angry, but it didn't. Evan was barely cognizant of the world around him. He lived to take care of the plants. He barely even looked at her when she was in the greenhouse. Which is how it should be. Lilly wanted her own space, and he gave it to her.

Tini emailed again yesterday, wondering where she was. Wanting to go out and see what kind of trouble they could get into. She also wanted to let her know that Asher Quinn had been asking about her. That had made her heart race, because Asher was... perfection. She hadn't realized he'd even noticed her at school. Lilly felt bad for not responding, but she didn't have answers Tini would want to hear. 'Hey, girl, yeah, I'm locked up in this super secure building outside of D.C. Nope, can't go trolling tonight...'

Her life sucked. She missed her friend.

The wind shifted and she looked up. There was nothing in front of her, but she thought she heard... She glanced around, aware that something was not right. Her heartbeat picked up, and the hair on her neck prickled. She couldn't tell where the fear came from, though.

A hand clamped over her mouth, and Lilly fought not to scream. She almost started fighting, but there was a light 'shhh' in her ear, and the arms dragged her back into the foliage of a large banana palm. She held still, wondering what Evan had seen that she hadn't. The fronds of the palm seemed to envelop them, leaving a small window to look out.

Within seconds, she knew. A tiny little black drone buzzed into the area, bouncing back and forth between the plants. It was so small it almost looked like a bee. It was obviously a machine, though. How long had it been watching them?

Evan held completely still behind her, barely breathing, and Lilly tried to match him. Man, if her mom knew that someone was watching her, her head might explode.

They watched the drone circle the greenhouse. Once, it hovered right in front of the banana tree, and Lilly had no idea how it didn't see them.

Then her mother stormed onto the scene, dark hair flying from the bun at the nape of her neck, her eyes furious.

Lilly should have known her mom would be on top of the situation. The infamous Belladonna walked into the greenhouse, looked at the drone, and made a crushing motion with her hand. Just that quickly, the threat was gone.

Evan let her go and they walked out from the tree. Her mother seemed startled to see her, and she looked at Evan with quiet consideration. "Thank you for hiding my daughter."

Without a word or a look at Lilly, Evan turned and went into the depths of the greenhouse.

Mom wrapped her arms around Lilly, and she let her, curling into her mother's embrace. Mom didn't hug her often, and Lilly missed it. She understood it was because of the senator, and what he'd done to her, but she missed the affection. Lilly thought she'd been raped, although Mom never came out and told her that for sure. Lilly just knew that the woman from before four years ago and the woman now were very different.

Mom drew back, looking into her eyes. "Are you okay?"

"Evan kept me safe," she said, nodding.

Mom looked back at the banana tree. Lilly followed her gaze. Yeah, they should have been seen there. Lilly frowned. It was full, but not that full. How had he hidden her there?

"When I came up, I didn't see you," Mom told her. "The leaves hid the two of you completely."

Donna moved over to the tiny drone. It had fallen into a fern. She wrapped a hand around it and stuck it in the pocket of her tan pants.

"Let's go inside."

Uh oh. That was the MOM voice. If she didn't nip this in the bud, she was going to take the only outside refuge she had away. "Mom, I'm fine. I don't think the drone even saw me."

"Well, I know it won't see you inside."

Lilly pulled to a stop. "I can't live in a bubble, Mom. You're not taking this away from me."

Her mother's expression hardened. "If it's for your safety, I most certainly can."

"No, Mom," she said, standing firm. "I won't be a prisoner again."

That finally seemed to stop her. She blinked, her dark brows furrowing. "It's not the same."

"To me it is," Lilly said softly, though she hated comparing the two situations. "I know I was being held captive and under guard, but at least at the Senator's house I had friends from school I could talk to on the phone and places I could go. I'm not used to literally being in one single building my entire life. This greenhouse is the only refuge I have. It's the only one you've given me."

Tears filled her mother's eyes. "I never meant for you to feel like that, Lilly-bean."

Lilly smiled slightly at the pet-name. "But I do."

Donna sighed, and pulled her into her arms. Lilly took

the second hug, resting her head against her mother's neck. She wasn't quite as tall, but she was getting there. When she pulled back, Donna was clear-eyed again. "I'll try to get you a phone, something we can keep track of but no one else can."

The thought of having that little bit of realness brought tears to her own eyes. "Thanks, Mom."

"Now, let's go inside and give this drone to one of the tech guys to see what he can get from it."

They walked to the elevator together. Lilly glanced back at one point, and Evan was there, watching her. She gave him a little wave of thanks, and he turned away.

## 3

H aven and three of the security team met Donna and Lilly on the elevator.

"What happened?" he asked, fear in his throat as he thought about her confronting anyone. Or anything.

Donna reached into her pocket and retrieved a pile of black plastic and metal, handing it over. Haven immediately recognized it as a drone. "Where was this?"

"Inside the greenhouse."

Haven looked at Lilly. "Are you okay?"

The girl nodded, leaning into her mother's side. She did seem fine, though her lips were pinched. "I don't think it even saw me. Evan hid me before it could."

Haven blinked and smiled slightly. Good. He'd thought Evan would step up if the situation presented itself. Obviously, the former Marine was more aware than he let on.

Haven turned the tiny drone in his hands. Yep, there was the camera. "Did you have to crunch it?"

Donna shrugged, grimacing slightly.

"Thanks for not destroying the lithium battery, at least. That would have corrupted everything." He handed the drone to Copper. "Run that to the tech lab, will you, and see what they can get from it."

The big guard nodded and punched the button for the sixth floor, then moved to the corner. Copper didn't like anything moving beneath his feet, so the elevator was a challenge. He only used it if the situation was time-sensitive, like today. When Donna had bolted for the elevator, only one of the floor guards had seen her, but he'd immediately put a call through to Haven, then the rest of the team. As Team Leader, he'd put out an order that he was to be advised of every situation dealing with Donna or Lilly, no matter the time or situation. If Donna was left to deal with things, he would never know what was going on. She was so damned close to the chest with everything.

"We'll have Krammer take a look at it and see if it's still transmitting."

"I don't think it is," Donna murmured. She glanced at Lilly. "Did you see any others up there? Or hear anything else?"

Lilly shook her dark head. Her hair was pulled back in a messy pony-tail, but he thought she'd made it that way on purpose. Her makeup was done, though she wasn't going anywhere, her lashes dark with mascara. Did sixteen year-olds always put make-up on when they were going to a greenhouse? He had no idea. Probably? He asked Donna, mentally, and she grinned slightly.

*Yes, make-up has to be done if she's anywhere other than the apartment or the workout room.*

*In case a wandering teenage boy sees her?*

The grin widened and she had to turn her face away. *Yes, just in case.*

Haven heaved a mental sigh. *Oh, to be young again.*

Donna's face fell, and the feeling between them changed. Haven cursed himself. *Sorry, Donna.*

*You're fine, Haven. Sometimes we just can't help but yearn...*

That was so true.

"Let's head downstairs. I'm sure Wulfe will want to hear about this. You can return to your posts," he told the team.

The guards disbursed and Haven escorted Lilly and Donna down to Wulfe's office. When he knocked on the cracked door, Elizabeth answered.

"What happened," she asked as she ushered them into the room.

Lilly liked Dr. Cole, so she immediately went in for a hug. "There was someone watching us. Or trying to."

Elizabeth hugged the girl, then set her back. "Are you okay?"

Lilly nodded. "Yeah. I didn't really realize what was going on until Evan pulled me back and hid me."

Haven met Wulfe's hard stare. *We thought he would step up when needed, and he did.*

Wulfe gave a single nod. *Good to know.*

*Krammer has the drone now.*

*Good.*

*They're stepping up the surveillance.*

*Yes, they are. Getting ballsy. We're going to have to go on the offensive. I have a couple of things in the works. And Kevin Rose is investigating. I'm tired of feeling like we're under a microscope.*

*God, yes,* Haven agreed. *It needs to stop.*

The women were still talking, and he took a moment to watch Donna. She seemed reserved around Elizabeth, and he wasn't sure why, exactly. They'd worked together a lot since Donna had been liberated from the senator. Haven knew that she was down on the hospital floor every day. If the patient had a mental issue or a block, Donna could work on them. And she could encourage whatever mental ability they had. Haven knew for a fact that he wouldn't be nearly as useful as he was now if it hadn't been for her help. It was like she removed the bandage that was restricting his movement. After they were done with their sessions, he felt reborn. It was an incredible feeling.

It also made him uncomfortable, because he had a certain... affection for Donna. And he was sure she knew about it because she was literally tinkering in his brain, but she never said anything. And she certainly never acted upon it. When the weaker telepaths had 'leaks', the stronger telepaths very politely tried to ignore them.

One of the first things all residents did when they were able was to work on their mental shields. They had several strong telepaths in the building, and every day they had conditioning exercises to both build and maintain strong shields. The stronger telepaths challenged those with the weaker shields, making everyone stronger.

Even those without mental abilities were taught to envision creating a mental shield around their mind. And for the most part, it worked, as long as they believed it worked. Dr. Cole had not been given any of the drug, but because she worked with many telepaths who could either deliberately or accidentally read her mind and emotions, Wulfe had been training her to wall off her mind. Haven used to pick up a lot from her 'public' mind, thoughts she almost voiced out loud, but he didn't very often any more.

Training the mental abilities was as important as anything to do with the physical, maybe even more so.

Haven sighed, feeling a little out of sorts. He was building a home here. He had money in the bank- a significant amount actually- but he was restless for more. After what he'd been through he deserved more, but there were certain things he couldn't make happen. Like make Donna look at him as more than a guard or a resident.

∽

AS SOON AS the drone died, Keith Kenney slammed the lid shut on his laptop and shoved it into the backpack. Then he grabbed the water bottle he'd emptied and the sub sandwich wrapper, shoving them into the pack as well. Leave no trace behind. His phone buzzed in his pocket and he knew who it was, but he didn't want to take the time to answer it. Because he knew what the man would say.

He was in such deep shit.

Kenney had been watching the Elton Recovery building for weeks, looking for weaknesses, but there were few. The building was locked down, and a guard at a gate controlled who got into the parking garage. A person could walk into the lobby, but there appeared to be three layers of security to even talk to someone. The only slight break in their security was on the roof, at the greenhouse. It covered most of the rooftop, and he'd noticed it from aerial photos. The Elton Recovery building stood on its own, though. No power lines connected to the next building, or shared walls. It was a self-sufficient island unto itself.

Closing the door behind himself, he jogged down the stairs to the bottom floor, eyes peeled for anything out of the ordinary. This building was vacant, though, and had been slated to be demolished for a while. He let himself through the front door, then crossed to the chain link fence. He tried to push the gate pieces together, but it hung open a little drunkenly. If they really looked, they could probably find where he'd been hanging out.

The drone had been a serious loss. McCullough had told him to watch the roof, but he'd gotten impatient. Kenney was man enough to admit that he'd acted rashly, but he thought he'd seen a young girl. If she was being held captive, they needed to know.

His phone buzzed again, and he yanked it from his pocket. He paused along the wall of the building, glancing around. It was late afternoon, and no one was around. Swallowing, he swiped his thumb across the screen.

"What the fuck were you thinking?"

Kenney winced at McCullough's angry voice. "I know, I know... I'm sorry. I got over-enthusiastic."

"Are you kidding me right now? That was more than 'over-enthusiastic'. You fucking outed us, Kenney."

He couldn't argue with McCullough's fury. He really had bungled it, and now the enemy had the drone. "They won't get anything off of it. By the time they figure out the GPS feature, I'll be long gone."

"Yeah, you will be."

That was the last thing Keith Kenney ever heard.

DEXTER CHASE COCKED HIS HEAD, wondering if that had been what he'd thought it was. That faint sound on the air had sounded like a gunshot. He'd heard more than one silenced weapon in his life, and the *pfft* sound was very unique.

He sauntered along the sidewalk three blocks from the Dog Pound, dragging in great draughts of cold air. It was a crisp day outside, with the sun going down. He'd heard through the earpiece that they'd taken a drone down on the roof, and it was his job to see what was hiding outside.

This part of the city was still industrial, but comforts were moving in. He could walk to a Starbucks now, just a few blocks away, and breathe in the scent. He wasn't much of a coffee drinker, but it was true that coffee beans were a palate cleanser. It cleared the lingering scents in his nasal passages like nothing else.

Dex paused, his head swiveling. Bending down, he pretended to tie his boot. He drew in a deep breath. That was blood he smelled. He turned his head slightly. It was coming from the east.

Wulfe had said to watch for anything out of the ordinary. Well, blood was definitely out of the ordinary.

Dex settled back into his saunter. He keyed the tiny mic at his ear. "Bad Dog Three to Bad Dog One."

There was an instant of static. "Go ahead, Bad Dog Three."

"I've got blood in the air. Repeat, blood in the air. Scouting east."

"Copy that Bad Dog Three."

HAVEN HEARD THE RADIO CALL, and his senses immediately went on alert. It could mean anything, though. Dex's sense of smell was pretty incredible, so he could be picking up a homeless person who cut his hand, or even a dog that was killed on the road. Anything blood related. He would wait and see what he came up with.

Copper entered the room, with Jabari on his heels, probably assuming that they would be called to go out. Copper, or Jake Pennyrile, was easily the strongest of the men in the building. He was a former Marine, pale blond haired and pale blue-eyed, and he'd been liberated from the Guyana camp. Noah Cross had fought him in the ring several times, and had to concede defeat. The crazy thing was, Copper was big, but he wasn't stacked with muscle like Noah was. His mind, though, told him he was stronger than anyone else, and his body believed it.

Jabari had been a part of the South African Special Forces Brigade, and they'd found him at a camp in Egypt just a few months ago. He'd been malnourished to the point that he'd been a pile of bones, and he was still regaining the weight.

There was a lean, dangerous air to him, though, and he moved like he was on the hunt. He was another guard who could fade into the shadows. He wasn't as good as concealing himself as Haven was, but his dark skin disappeared into any hint of shadow.

They were both kitted out in a version of the US Army uniform; black tactical shirt, black BDU pants and boots. And they'd been given combat vests, chest rigs, and holsters to mount their weapons. It was their everyday attire, and Haven felt naked if he wasn't in his uniform.

Haven, Dex, Copper and Jabari made up Fire Team 4. They did everything together. All ops they were sent on, they were sent as a group, usually. They trained together and ate together, and their rooms were in the same block upstairs.

As the men on the hospital floors recovered, they were asked what they wanted to do. If they wanted to return to their home country, they were allowed, though the Dogs could not guarantee their welcome when they returned to their own country. Under their agreement with the CIA and General Holtman, any man that wanted to stay in the country would receive a visa to work with the Dogs of War and Joint Task Force Omega. Just like signing up for the military, they were signed to a four-year commitment, with the option to re-enlist. The men that joined were paid well. Better than many of them had been paid before.

They had liberated eight men from six different countries from the African continent. The African soldiers had all been labelled deserters by their home country once the Dogs of War had stolen them from the torture camps. Haven was still scratching his head over that one. They were expected to stay and be tortured for their military. But because they aren't being tortured anymore, their country had disavowed them. The eight Africans had no recourse but to stay and make a life here.

The other men from that camp were here, and negotiations were going on with their countries in relation to their individual service records. Every camp they'd raided had housed soldiers and operators from multiple countries. Ideally, Joint Task Force Omega would 'appreciate' the release of those soldiers from their military contracts, so that they could stay in the states. Three men liberated from the Guyana camp had been from the Soviet Union, and they'd had to return to their countries. Haven hated to think what had happened to them. They'd either been killed or had been folded into their own enhanced-soldier program. It was assumed that every major political power had their own version of the program.

Dr. Cole had found the agreements Dr. Shu and Damon Wilkes had made with the individual countries, and per the contract, the men or bodies were supposed to be returned to the originating country once testing had been completed. Shu had been greedy, though, and those that died in the camps had been autopsied, and multiple samples collected. Then the carcass, as he called the former soldiers, had been returned to their home countries.

It had been barbaric in the extreme. Valuable special forces soldiers had been reduced to bags of bones. The waste of good talent was horrific.

The earpiece clicked. "You might wanna just ride this way, Bad Dog One."

Immediately, Haven was on the move, his men following him. They headed to the garage, and Copper snagged the key fob for one of the suburbans. They piled in and he started the vehicle. There were two gates to get up out of the building's basement, and though Haven appreciated the security, he hated the time it took them to get out of the building. As soon as they were street level he expanded his senses, pointing in the direction he felt Dex. Copper turned the wheel and accelerated down the block, then turned right when Haven pointed. They were only three blocks away when they spotted Dex, leaning over what looked to be a body.

Copper pulled into the alley and parked at an angle. Hopefully, it would be enough to block anyone from seeing them as they checked the body and surroundings.

Haven scanned the area as he slipped out of the vehicle, his hand hovering over his weapon. He knew the other two men were being just as cautious.

"What do you know," he asked Dex as he stopped near the body.

It was a younger man, mid-thirties maybe- with thick brown hair. He was dressed in jeans, a rock band tee he didn't recognize, and a thick jacket. And there was a perfect, round bullet-hole through the middle of his forehead.

"Well, he was alive less than ten minutes ago," Dex said grimly. "Lividity hasn't even begun to set in."

Haven pulled his phone out and snapped a couple of pictures, then leaned close for a full face pic. He immediately sent it to Aiden. *Dead body 3 blocks from Dog Pound. Former drone operator?*

*I'll see what I can dig up about him.*

"Can you track his backtrail," Haven asked Dex.

Dex lifted his head to the wind and nodded. "Definitely. There's another scent, here, too. I assume it's the shooter."

"Recognize it?"

Dex shook his head. "It's no one I've met in the past year."

Haven took him at his word. Dex had been placed into service about six months ago and he hadn't been out as much as some of them. He had an incredible scent library in his brain, and he could permanently remember a scent after only catching it once.

"Can you tell if this guy was enhanced?"

"Yup. Though he smells off, like it didn't take right."

Haven nodded, logging the information in his brain. He had a feeling they would find a service record for the guy. Leaning down, he shifted the jacket until he could see the skin of his shoulders. "Former Marine, it looks like."

Copper grunted behind him, and he stepped closer. "No one I recognize," he murmured. "What's the tat?"

Haven showed him. There were no identifying words other than *Semper Fidelis* in a strange stencil font.

"Hm," Copper grumbled.

Haven snorted. Copper didn't like not having more information. And neither did he. "Let's follow the back-trail. Jabari, scout around, see if you can see anything."

Jabari headed down the alley, and the three of them headed toward the main street. Dex followed the scent around the corner to the front of an old, derelict apartment building, and up several flights of stairs. At the top floor he turned left, and pushed open the hanging door of an apartment. It was obvious someone had been in here. The table had been pushed near the open window, and a chair sat behind it.

"Where is the controller of the drone?" Haven murmured.

"Haven't seen it," Dex said, pacing the area. "He was here for several days. And slept over there." He made a motion with his hand to a pallet on the floor against the far wall. "No other scents."

Haven moved to the window. The view gave him a sightline to the Elton Building roof. Not close enough to see inside the greenhouse or anything, but close enough to see anyone on the roof itself.

"What's the plan?" Copper asked, his hand on his weapon.

Haven took a deep breath and let it out slowly. "We need to find the controller of that drone. And we need to find out who killed this guy and why."

"I'll start running facial recognition and checking for any

suspicious activity in the area," Aiden's voice came through on Haven's earpiece.

"Good. Dex, can you pick up any other scents in the area?"

Dex nodded and started sniffing the air. "There's a faint smell of gasoline, and something else. Can't quite place it."

He keyed his mic. "Jabari, you seeing anything?"

"No," Jabari said. "Nothing out of the ordinary."

Haven thought for a moment. "Let's split up. Dex, follow the scent of gasoline and see where it leads. Copper, you're with me. We're going to search the rest of this building and see if we can find anything else."

The team split up and went their separate ways. Haven and Copper started searching the apartment, looking for anything that might give them a clue as to what happened here. They checked the pallet where the victim had been sleeping, but there was nothing there except a blanket and a pillow. "Check the table," Copper said, pointing to the pushed-aside furniture. Haven moved closer and saw that there was a tablet sitting on the table. He opened it and saw that it was password-protected.

"Can you hack it?" Copper asked.

"No, but Aiden or Krammer can." He slipped it into one of the cargo pockets of his BDUs.

At that moment, Jabari's voice came through on their earpieces. "I found something. You guys need to see this."

Haven followed his mental trail down through the building, across two blocks and back up into another building. They exited on the roof, and saw Jabari standing a few yards away. "This is where the shooter was."

Haven looked at the ledge. There was the slightest of scrapes, but it was nothing obvious. Just a faint lightening in the concrete brick. He keyed his mic. "Dex, can you come up here?"

"Yes, sir."

Within two minutes he was there, puffing a little from running the stairs. He nodded as soon as he got there. "Yes, sir, this is definitely the shooter."

Haven keyed his mic again. "Warden, can you access any CCTV around here?"

"There isn't much, Bad Dog One," Aiden said, voice low. "I've been looking."

"Maybe it would be beneficial for us to add our own in a few places," Haven murmured.

"Agreed," Aiden murmured, and Haven knew Wulfe would have cameras up within hours. It was probably something they should have already done.

"Where did the gas smell lead to," he asked Dex.

"To an old beater Jeep a couple blocks away. It's already been gutted by the guy I smell up here."

Haven sighed, knowing they were at a dead end. The only recourse they had was to find them through records search or catch them on surveillance.

Haven took a swab of the man's blood before they called in an anonymous tip that he had been found. Hopefully, the sample would be enough to tell Dr. Cole if the man was enhanced or not. He trusted Dex's nose, but it was good to have scientific proof, as well.

"Let's head back," he said, heading for the Suburban. They didn't want to be there when the cops arrived.

# 4

Donna moved through the building quietly, not making eye contact with anyone. She was restless and needed to move, but had no destination.

Haven was outside the building, and she was on edge. When he'd been gone in Colorado, her nerves had been at the breaking point. Haven... reassured her. They'd had an incident today, and she had a feeling they would be having more in the future. Lilly was fine, but she knew her daughter was chafing at the control she was under. And Donna couldn't blame her. No sixteen-year-old girl wanted to be locked up in a building like this, with tormented men who cried out almost nightly. What were the options, though?

If she had to, she could bug out. *They* could bug out. She had some money stashed away, and she was confident in her ability to manipulate a situation. If she had to, she could *finesse* people, as Wulfe liked to call it. Make them see more money than was in their hand and the like. She wouldn't do that unless it was an emergency situation, though. No one should have their mind manipulated against their knowledge.

Dr. Cole and the Dogs of War had given her a purpose, and a home. She wasn't free, per se, but she agreed to stay under their roof for their protection. For Lilly's sake.

And because it was better than being snatched by one of senator Hall's cronies. Yes, the odious man was in prison, but she knew he wanted her back. She had been an integral part of their testing regime. She was the one who gave the go-ahead, or not, on the soldiers. There was something in her that knew if the drug would work on a soldier. And she had been able to sense the slightest variations in the serum.

Before she'd been dosed herself, she'd been a nurse in the Army at Fort Benning, Georgia. It had been a profession she'd loved, and she'd been exceptional at it. Four years ago, she'd heard about a job opening. It was a research opportunity looking for especially intuitive people. Donna felt like she fit that description. She would still be in the Army, but the clinical trial was to enhance empathy. At the time, Donna remembered thinking if she understood the patient's issues more fully, she could be a better nurse. After thinking about it for a couple of days, she had gone to Dr. Shu's office. The man had been brilliant, and she'd been fascinated as he'd described the process he'd gone through to refine the ayahuasca. The science had been revolutionary, so she'd jumped in with both feet. It had only been later when she'd seen the edge of madness creeping into Dr. Shu's work. He'd chafed at the Army's restrictions, and somehow he'd managed to get permission to create an off-site facility. Even back then he was wheeling and dealing with people in power.

In the backwoods of Georgia, they'd settled into a warehouse and started expanded testing. At that time, about three months after she'd gotten her first injection, Donna was feeling strong. She was working part time at the hospital on base, and the rest of the time with Dr. Shu at the off-base facility. The first month, the drug had caused migraines, severe enough that she'd passed out from the pain. Then Dr. Shu had found a variation of the formula that didn't cause migraines as bad, and after the second shot, Donna had felt herself start to grow. She began picking up impressions from the surrounding people, and she knew when a patient was going to crash. She'd always been an intuitive nurse, but once she'd started taking the drug, her abilities grew by leaps and bounds. Dr. Shu kept her at the Georgia location only after a few months, and that was when the madness began to take over. The more successes he had, the more driven he became.

Dr. Edgar Shu was brilliant, and looking back, she realized he had probably been on the autistic spectrum. The man had had no people skills, and he'd left it up to her to pave the way for whatever was coming with the volunteers. At the time, they'd only had about twenty participants in the trials, and Shu had been motivated to produce results, even to the point of the participant's pain. Donna wasn't sure who had been motivating the doctor at that time, but she could see the pressure the man was under.

Donna blinked and looked around, a little lost. She was in one of the rec rooms. She moved to the window, looking out at the night. Her mind was still racing, clicking through faces of men she'd lost. Sergeant Charles White had been the first for a lot of reasons. As a communications interceptor, he listened to radio transmissions all day, every day. Once he'd been given the serum, his hearing had gotten so enhanced that he'd gone crazy. Literally. He heard sounds from miles away, and at the time there had been no way to guard him against what he'd gained. Within four days of receiving his second shot, he'd committed suicide.

At the time, the men had been returning to base for their

regular shifts, and doing the experiments in their off-time. After Charles' suicide, Dr. Shu had gotten permission to keep the men on-site, under observation. He slept at the facility as well, and he began to turn in on himself. Donna and a few other nurses took care of the men, until the doctor would come out with some new variation.

Besides Charles, they had several 'successes' early on. There was Private First Class Jack Johnson, who had been a complete adrenaline junkie before the experiments. He would always be the first to volunteer for anything dangerous, and he had the scars to prove it. After receiving the serum, Jack's reflexes had become so heightened that he could anticipate everyone's movement. It was almost like he had a sixth sense, and they had been thrilled with the results. Jack had never been happier. But after a few months, he began to experience seizures. The heightened senses were too much for his brain to handle, and it had shut down. Jack had died in his sleep, only a few days after his second injection.

There was one soldier, Private White, who had become so strong that he had ripped apart his restraints and attacked the staff. They had to lock him in a room until they could figure out what to do with him. And then there was Private Thompson, who had developed an insatiable hunger that the doctors couldn't control. They had to keep him sedated at all times.

When word got out about the failures, the brass had shut them down. They had still been under military oversight. As far as she knew, Private Thompson was still in a medically induced coma at Fort Benning, and White was still in the brig. Dr. Shu's experiments had shown enough promise, though, that he'd gained the backing of Senator Cameron Hall and several wealthy private businessmen, Dr. Cole's ex-husband included. Shu had gotten the backing that he'd needed to move the experiments out of the country, and away from the control of the brass. She hadn't wanted to leave the country. At the time, her ex-husband had had Lilly with him in Virginia. It was hard enough getting to see her daughter while stationed in Georgia. Donna couldn't imagine trying to see her when she was out of the country. So, she'd dragged her feet. Shu had offered her a huge bonus, though, for continuing with the project. It was more money than she'd ever even dreamed of making in the Army, and it would secure Lilly's future. So, she'd agreed. That had been almost a year into the testing.

Shu didn't keep her in the loop on everything, and she was surprised and horrified when they'd landed at the first camp in Brazil. There were more men here than they'd ever experimented on before, and it was obvious a lot had been going on behind the scenes while she'd been dragging her feet. When she arrived, the men were grumbling about the accommodations. She didn't blame them. They were living in bug-infested, over-capacity dorms, and the men had no room. The participants were also from countries from all over the world, so there was friction as they tried to get along with each other. And with the new move had come less medical restrictions. Shu was using more and more variations of the ayahuasca serum, and men were dying horrible deaths. She tried to get him to slow down and be more conscientious of what they were doing, but the mania was gaining ground. Eventually he settled on one variation of the drug that seemed to enhance anyone it was given to. That had been Spartan.

Donna's heart was heavy as she remembered the chaos and destruction that had followed. She had witnessed men who had been transformed into machines, their humanity stripped away as they lost themselves. She had seen others go mad, consumed by the heightened senses and the overwhelming power that came with the serum. Shu had hired local militia to keep them in line.

As the days passed, the situation at the camp only seemed to get worse. The men were becoming more agitated and restless, and the friction between the participants from different countries was turning into open hostility. The overcrowded living conditions weren't helping matters, and the lack of proper medical care was taking its toll. She worked from sun up to sun down, taking care of sick men. The jungle itself created more problems. Eventually, there was a rebellion. That was when the men had been placed in literal cages, like lions at a zoo. The living conditions had been horrific, and she'd argued vehemently against them. She'd even gone so far as to threaten to go to the authorities. Who that would have been, she didn't know. Because the country that was hosting the camp got a very large kickback for turning a blind eye.

She remembered that conversation very clearly. Dr. Shu had looked at her like she was a traitor, and that was when he'd informed her that there had been a terrible accident. Her ex-husband had been killed, and Lilly was now under the care of Senator Cameron Hall.

Donna could still remember the sense of shock that had rolled through her, and the paralyzing fear. Her life was no longer her own, and to ensure Lilly's safety, she raised no further objections. She read the writing on the wall quite clearly.

Donna had watched Dr. Shu become more and more erratic in his behavior. He seemed to be driven by a manic energy, and he was using increasingly dangerous doses of the ayahuasca serum in his experiments. She tried to reason with him, to make him see the risks of what they were doing, but he wouldn't listen. He was obsessed with the idea of unlocking the full potential of the human mind, and he believed the ends justified the means.

She remembered feeling like she was in a nightmare that she couldn't wake up from. She was imprisoned in a remote jungle camp with a group of volatile and unpredictable men, and she was partially responsible for overseeing experiments that were spiraling out of control. The sheer stupidity of what she'd done, what she'd involved herself in, boggled her mind.

Shu created more camps, with more military 'volunteers'. And more men died. She tried to narrow down exactly what it was that would allow one soldier to live, and another to die, but she couldn't always tell. When she touched the men, she could just feel whether or not the ayahuasca would work with the man's mind or not. Sometimes Shu took her advice, other times he didn't. Thinking back, she thought he chose to use the ones she'd weeded out just to spite her with their horrible deaths.

She knew that she had to do something to stop Dr. Shu before it was too late. But what could she do? She didn't have the authority to shut down the experiments, and she didn't have the power to make Dr. Shu listen to reason.

As the situation at the camp continued to deteriorate, Donna feared they were all headed toward a catastrophic end. She knew that something had to be done, but she didn't know what. All she could do was wait and hope that someone, somewhere, would intervene before it was too late.

Luckily, a viper took care of the madman. Unfortunately for her, there was more than one madman. Within days of Dr. Shu dying in the jungle, Senator Hall had arrived to 'save' her. He'd known how valuable she was from his previous interactions with Shu, and no matter how much she pleaded, he would not let her or Lilly go. "You have a responsibility to help these men," he'd said, waving a hand at the surrounding cages.

Donna had bowed her head to him to keep him from seeing the fury in her heart, but it was as if he'd known. He'd taken her into custody and fitted her with the collar, as if she were a dog. She'd never been more humiliated in her life, and she'd vowed that she would make it out with her daughter, and she would kill as many men as she had to, including the senator.

It was her greatest regret, that she hadn't had the chance to kill the senator. So many of their problems would resolve themselves if he were gone.

Donna shook her head, trying to push the memories away. The past tended to swallow her. She couldn't afford to lose focus, not when there was so much at stake now. She needed to be present, and help Lilly settle into the life they'd been given. Turning away from the window, she made her way back out into the hallway, her footsteps echoing through the quiet building. She wasn't even sure exactly where she was.

A nurse in maroon scrubs turned the corner in front of her, and she smiled when she saw Donna. "Donna. Did you follow your nose to the fresh cookies?"

Donna gave Raine a slight smile, and lifted her head. There *was* a fresh chocolate scent in the air. "I didn't think so, but maybe I did."

Raine's grin widened, and she nodded conspiratorially. Donna liked Raine. She was an excellent nurse, and she very obviously cared for the men on her floor. She'd taken care of Haven when he'd been here. Donna glanced around again. Yes, she was on the fourth floor.

"Come on, we'll share."

Donna followed along, feeling like she needed to talk to someone. She wasn't sure she wanted a cookie, but she appreciated Raine's mood. The woman was perpetually optimistic.

Raine led her to the staff break room. There was a petite

young girl with dark hair moving behind the island, setting plates of cookies out from a wheeled cart. She smiled when Raine entered the room, and Donna realized she wasn't a young girl, but a woman in her thirties. Her diminutive size had deceived Donna. Instinctively, she reached out mentally, doing a risk assessment, but the woman was not a danger. On the contrary, she was absolutely terrified to be here.

"Donna, this is Nicolette," Raine said, making a wave with her hand. "She's the baker that pumps all the delicious smells through the building, and feeds us so well. I swear, Nic, I've gained ten pounds since I've started working here."

Nic smiled, though her dark green eyes danced fearfully to Donna. Without being obvious, she moved to place the cart between Donna and herself.

Donna was used to the reaction. For many years, she had been Belladonna, killer of the weak and defenseless. Or at least, that had been the way she'd been portrayed. She'd never actually killed anyone. Well... no one that didn't need killing. Her reputation had gotten around, apparently.

She gave Nicolette a slight smile. "Thank you for the deliciousness. My daughter loves your cookies."

Nic's expression lightened a little, but she still looked like she wanted to get out of the room as fast as humanly possible. "I'm glad," she murmured. "Lilly is a great kid."

Donna focused more intently on Nic. "You've met her?"

Nic, looking like a rabbit about to bolt, nodded. "She comes down to the kitchen occasionally, looking for something to do. Sometimes I put her to work. I hope you don't mind."

Her voice wavered at the end, and Donna felt bad for making the woman so fearful. Deliberately, she eased her expression into a smile, and loosened her posture. "No, I don't mind. I know she's struggling here." Moving forward, she reached for a cookie. "These are fantastic, by the way."

"Thank you." Nic positioned herself behind the cart. "If you'll excuse me. Bye, Raine."

"Bye, Nic," Raine murmured, mouth already full of cookie.

The two of them watched as Nic escaped the break room, cart wheels rattling.

"Nic has been here longer than I have," Raine murmured, looking Donna in the eye. "She's a very nice lady with a sad history. Lilly is safe with her."

Donna sighed, looking down at the cookie in her hand. "I know. I'm just on edge."

"Noah stopped by and told me about the drone. Is Lilly okay?"

"Yes," Donna sighed, glancing up again to meet her friend's eyes. "But I instinctively want to clamp down on her."

"Well, of course you do," Raine murmured. "She's your kid. And with your history, it's completely understandable."

Each of them grabbed a spare cookie and a napkin, then moved to sit at one of the tables. Donna smiled slightly at Raine's enthusiasm for the sweets.

"I just don't know how to protect her," she said, finally voicing her biggest fear.

Raine looked up, her blue eyes narrowed with laughter. "You know you can only protect her so much."

"I know," Donna sighed, breaking off a piece of cookie. "I was separated from her for so long. I missed out on a lot of her changes. And I'm terrified she'll be taken from me again."

Donna hated to admit that, but she thought Raine would understand. The young nurse reached across the table and rested her hand on Donna's. "I know. And it's a very real possibility." She glanced back toward the floor. "The men that did this to these men are probably desperate to find you, and have leverage over you. They've killed more people in their greed than we will ever know. You, personally, have seen them work. I have no doubt they would use Lilly against you again, if they could."

Donna's heart sank as she heard those words. Raine was right, she had seen the cruelty of those men first-hand. They had already taken so much from her, and the thought of losing Lilly was unbearable. She took a deep breath and tried to compose herself. She couldn't let her fear control her. "But what can I do?" Donna asked, her voice barely above a whisper.

Raine squeezed her hand. "You can't control everything, but you can be prepared. You can make sure you have a plan in place, and that you and Lilly are both aware of it. You can teach her to be cautious and aware of her surroundings. And most importantly, you can love her and cherish every moment you have together."

Donna nodded. She hadn't known Raine long— a little over a year— but she always seemed to know what to say. "Thank you, Raine. I know I'm not rational about this."

"I wouldn't be either, if it was my kid. I heard they tried for baby Fallon in Denver."

Donna nodded. She hadn't been there, but she could imagine the fear Angela had gone through.

"I don't think Haven would have let anything happen to that baby," Raine said, licking chocolate off one finger. "I need milk. You want a glass?"

"Almond milk, please."

She watched Raine retrieve two glasses of almond milk and return to the table. She also grabbed the plate of cookies and set it on the table between them. "Still trying to care for me, Nurse Raine?"

Raine grinned, and shrugged lightly as she settled into the seat. "What can I say. It's my calling. You've gained weight since you came in, but you need to gain more."

Yes, she knew she did, but sometimes the thought of

eating just never even entered her head. Donna deliberately picked up a cookie and took a small bite, savoring the sweet taste. "I know. It's just hard sometimes."

"I know it is," Raine said softly. "But you have to take care of yourself, for Lilly's sake. And for yours."

Donna nodded, knowing that Raine was right. She needed to be strong, for herself and for her daughter.

## 5

**H**aven didn't like the answers he was receiving. "There's no record of this guy anywhere?"

Aiden shook his head. "Not that I'm finding. I have a request in to Interpol, but who knows how long that could take."

Haven tried not to be aggravated. They hadn't spoken to the dead guy, so they had no idea what nationality he'd been. "Damn. Krammer find anything?"

Shaking his head, Aiden swiveled in the chair to face him. "It's American made, but that's all he knows. He's trying to delve into the GPS info now."

Haven paced away, hands in his pockets.

"Nothing, hmm?"

Haven turned as soon as he heard her voice. Donna stood in the doorway of Aiden's office, looking disappointed. But still beautiful. Her dark hair was pulled to the nape of her neck, her beautiful skin flawless. Haven clamped down on his surge of reaction, trying not to be so damn obvious. She didn't need to be bothered by his reaction to her right now.

Damn, it was hard turning away, though. When he'd

spoken to Walker, the counselor, he'd suggested that Haven had impressed upon Donna when she'd rescued him. Haven had scoffed at that, because he'd been around the block more than a few times. He was a mature man, and he'd had his share of physical and emotional relationships. Walker made him sound like he'd imprinted upon her like a damn duckling.

Donna was different. Haven would swear there was something more pulling him to her, some inner knowledge that they would be good together. Even though he knew she had zero interest in any kind of relationship, emotional or otherwise. Right now, she was rebuilding her relationship with her daughter and trying to make a place for herself here with the Dogs of War and the men they were helping. There was resistance on both those fronts, but she was working through it. And he would do his best to help her as much as he could. If that was as close as she would let him be, he would take it.

Haven sighed, rubbing a hand over his face. "Not yet. Aiden's still digging, but so far this ghost we're chasing doesn't seem to exist."

Donna folded her arms over her stomach, leaning against the doorframe. "That doesn't make any sense. He had to come from somewhere."

"Yeah, well, whoever he was, he covered his tracks well."

Haven couldn't keep the frustration out of his voice. They'd been chasing shadows for weeks now, trying to find leads on Hall and his co-conspirators. This dead man in the alley seemed their first solid clue—until he turned out to be a ghost.

"We'll figure it out, Haven."

He gave her a grim smile, wishing he shared her confidence. His gaze traced over her face, lingering on her lips for a heartbeat too long. He forced himself to turn away, breaking the connection before she noticed. The pull he felt toward Donna was almost magnetic, but she'd given no indication she felt anything romantic for him. And after the hell she'd been through, he didn't blame her. Still, his feelings refused to fade, as much as he tried to ignore them. Counseling helped, but Walker was right about one thing—his bond with Donna went deeper than logic.

"Haven?"

His gaze snapped to her, and he realized he'd been woolgathering. "Yes."

"Did you ask him about the phone?" Donna asked.

Haven shook his head. "I've been dealing with other things, Donna, sorry."

Donna nodded and turned to Aiden. "Would it be possible to get Lilly a phone? Something we can monitor? She's feeling very isolated and I would like her to reconnect with her friends, if possible."

Aiden nodded and turned to the desk, jotting a note down. "I think we can do that. I'll talk to Wulfe about it."

Donna seemed satisfied with that. She gave Haven one last penetrating look, then disappeared down the hallway.

Haven dragged in a sharp breath, his entire body tense. He had to get these emotions under control. "I'll be back in a few,'" he said, and he took off after Donna.

Her narrow back was just rounding the corner when he got to the hallway. Haven jogged to catch up with her. She glanced at him, surprised. "Was there something else?"

Haven fought not to feel aggravated at the attempted brushoff. "No. I just wanted to check on you. I know you had to be scared when you thought Lilly was in danger."

Donna paused in the hallway, frowning, her arms still crossed over her stomach. "You know, the fear didn't hit until later. At the time I was angry. I had to secure her safety at all costs. Then I was aggravated that someone would dare approach us here. They're getting desperate, though. I have a feeling they're still running tests, but because I'm not there, more men will be dying."

Haven scowled. "You know you can't take that responsibility on your shoulders. If there are men dying, it's at the hands of Hall and whoever he has running the show right now. It has nothing to do with you what they do moving forward."

She pursed her mouth, one side pinching in. "Yes, my mind knows that, but my heart aches at the thought of what might be going on. But my focus needs to be on Lilly right now."

"Yes," he agreed. "And she needs you now. You're literally the only link she has to anything."

"I know," she whispered. She looked down at the floor for a moment, then back up at him. Haven was stunned to see tears in her eyes, and he lifted a hand to her. "Thank you, Haven. I get a little lost in myself sometimes, so I appreciate you giving me focus."

Haven was surprised at that. He gave a bark of laughter. "Well, we're even then. You did it for me."

Then, she did something he never would have expected. She stepped forward and very lightly wrapped her arms around him.

Stunned, Haven wanted to wrap his arms around her and pull her tight, but with a gigantic force of will, he didn't. He allowed her to hug him, then let him go. He couldn't help but smile, though. "What was that for?"

Her cheeks went a little pink, and she waved a hand. "Just because. Don't make me regret it."

Haven laughed, and before she could back away, he dropped a light kiss to her forehead. "Well, there. That was just because, too."

Her cheeks went even darker, and she spun away. She marched down the hallway without a glance back at him.

Haven laughed softly, feeling just a glimmer of hope. Surely she wouldn't have reacted like that if she wasn't a tiny bit interested...

W ULFE CALLED him down to the office a couple hours later. He held a white bag out to Haven. "Both of the phones are charged and ready to go. They have heavy-duty cases on them, but I assume the girl will want something pretty. Just let me know and we can order it delivered."

Haven grinned, looking down into the bag. Donna hadn't asked for a phone, but Wulfe knew that if Lilly had one, her mother would need one as well. And maybe it would be handy to be able to get in contact with her. "Are our numbers in there?"

Wulfe gave him a look. "Of course they are. She has the entire phone book."

Haven laughed at the look, and held up his hands. "Just checking. Don't go all German on me."

Wulfe eased back in his chair. "I'm fighting on a lot of fronts right now."

"Anything I can do to help?"

Wulfe shook his dark head. "They're trying to call the Omega Team out for some ridiculous training exercise. I told them we were involved in another issue, right now, and we would be passing. They weren't pleased."

"Was it Braden?" Haven asked, voice wry. "He's been a pain in the ass recently."

Wulfe nodded, giving him a look. Haven understood the look. Throughout their military careers, no matter the branch, they'd all had to deal with men who thought they were better than the men under them. Lieutenant Colonel Ezekial Braden thought he was better than everyone he came in contact with. He led an elite Delta Force that was part of their Omega team, and he constantly tried to undermine the Dogs. Wulfe had spoken to General Holtman, but it was one of those things that needed to be worked out between the men. Braden was constantly trying to show his squadron's superiority, but it was never going to happen. The only way he could do that was if he cheated in some way, which he'd been known to do.

The Dogs of War who had decided to join Task Force Omega numbered at twenty-three. All of those twenty-three men had been medically cleared for duty, and all had enhancements or abilities that allowed them to get an advantage over the Delta Force guys they trained with. The Dogs were more than aware, though, that that gave them an unfair advantage. When they trained with the Deltas, very often they would muffle whatever enhancements they had and fight 'without enhancement', or WE. Only when they trained with each other could they use their enhancements, and then it was balls to the wall. They learned the most when training with each other, because they knew, at some point, they would clash with other enhanced mercenaries.

None of the Dogs liked Lt. Colonel Braden, but they had to deal with him. Wulfe had had the foresight to add into the contract when they created Joint Task Force Omega that each group has ultimate autonomy. If the Dogs of War didn't agree with an operation, Wulfe, their official leader, had the option to excuse them from the op. He'd been using the clause fairly regularly, recently, because Braden seemed determined to out them to the press, which was ridiculous, because he would be outing his own squadron as well. Haven had the niggling thought that Braden could be getting a kick-back from former Senator Hall, but it was just a thought.

Haven sighed, shifting the bag of phones to his other hand. "Well, we'll have to keep an eye on Braden. His obsession with discrediting us is suspicious, to say the least. Do you think we can talk to Holtman again?"

Wulfe shook his head. "Not yet. We have enough to deal with tracking down leads on Hall's remaining allies. I don't want further distraction from bureaucratic nonsense." His expression turned grim. "How is Donna holding up with this latest threat?"

"As well as can be expected. She's worried for Lilly, and angry we didn't foresee this move." Haven scrubbed a hand over his face. "I should have anticipated they would target Lilly to use as leverage. What kind of mother wouldn't do anything to protect her child?"

"Go to them," Wulfe said gently. "Reassure them both. And make sure you have eyes on Lilly at all times."

Haven nodded, resolve hardening within him. He would assign a protection detail to watch the floor whenever Donna had to leave. And he would visit as often as possible himself, to ensure their safety and comfort. The thought of Lilly being used as a weapon against her own mother made his blood boil. Hall and his goons had a lot to answer for.

Wulfe's voice broke into his furious thoughts. "Stay focused on the real threats here, not Braden's transparent agenda. Keep me posted if there are any developments or leads to follow."

Haven gave him a salute and left the office. Copper was in the hallway. Haven related the extra security rotation for Donna and Lilly. Copper nodded. "I expected that. I let squad four know we'd probably be needing them."

"Excellent." Haven clapped him on the back and headed for the elevator, bag swinging in his hand. Copper headed for the stairs. Haven was anxious to take the gadgets to the girls. Opening his senses just a little, he felt for Donna. Yep, she was in her apartment, and it felt like Lilly was too. Folding his hands, he waited for the elevator to deliver him.

When he knocked on the door, Lilly answered, which surprised him. Usually she was in her room, on her tablet. "Hey, Haven," she grinned. "Please tell me you have a pizza in that bag, or something super interesting."

Haven grinned, shaking his head. "Well, I don't know about a pizza, but it's interesting. I'll let your mom talk to you about it."

Lilly tilted her dark head, her dark blue eyes widening. "Oh, I'm curious now." She waved him in. "Mom's in the kitchen, burning soup."

Chuckling, Haven moved through the apartment. This was one of the biggest ones on the floor, because there were two of them living in it. It had two bedrooms, two baths, a good sized living room and a kitchen. Haven knew Donna had been trying to cook dinners for Lilly nightly, though he didn't think it was going well. Donna had been a nurse by trade, and her husband had had custody of their daughter while she'd been in the military, so she'd never had to cook for anyone, per se.

He stopped at the breakfast bar, and watched Donna stir a pot furiously. She glanced up at him, and grimaced. Some of her dark hair had fallen from her bun, and it wisped at the side of her face in the heat. "Hey, Haven. Just a minute."

Grinning, he sat on one of the stools, enjoying seeing her so flustered. Donna was the epitome of calm, cool and collected, and her feathers were vary rarely ruffled. He enjoyed seeing her this way, more normal, more human. Lilly brought that out in her.

For several months, when she'd first moved in here with Lilly, she had been incredibly reserved. She didn't socialize or do more than Dr. Cole required of her. Haven had very rarely seen her. Even when he'd asked, she'd refused to see him. Which had been hard, because his senses had been newly awakened, thanks to her, and he wanted to be able to tell her how much he appreciated what she'd done. She sensed the animosity from some of the other men in the building, though. They'd viewed her as the enemy for many years, and Haven had had to actively campaign for them to give her a chance. He was a walking, talking billboard for what she could do. Eventually, they'd given in and agreed to give her a chance.

To let her know, he'd sent her a letter, as crazy at that was living in the same building. He'd told her how much he appreciated what she'd done for him, and that he hoped she realized she would not be abused here. He'd also told her that the men in the building were willing to give her a chance. It had taken a week of silence. Then one day, he'd looked up from training and there she'd been, watching him practice. Copper had taken that inattention to lay him out on the mat, and when he'd looked over again, Donna had been gone.

She'd been more present, though, after that, and she'd started helping where she could. Aiden's wife Angela had been pregnant, and Donna had helped her through her chronic morning sickness and the pre-eclampsia. Then, one by one, some of the men came to her for help. Sometimes it was just to ease the PTSD symptoms. Sometimes it was more than that. Titus, one of the comatose patients on the fourth floor, seemed to be coming around a little. Donna had laid her hands on him several times, both to ease his pain and to sharpen his consciousness. As with every other soldier who had been given Spartan, Donna's innate and trained abilities were enhanced by the drug. And she seemed to still be growing stronger, even though the shots had stopped.

Then she'd started loosening up. One day he'd caught her laughing with Nurse Raine, and the picture was branded in his mind. She'd been so beautiful, her head tipped back and her mouth spread in a smile. Her eyes had been shining in a way that he hadn't seen before, and he was so glad that she was beginning to feel more comfortable.

Donna finally looked up from the pot, blowing a stray hair from her face. Her cheeks were flushed, and she looked adorably frustrated. Haven grinned. "Need some help?"

She sighed, shaking her head and stepping back from the stove. "I don't know why I thought I could make beef stew. I'm afraid it's burnt beyond saving."

Haven turned off the burner and peered into the pot, wincing at the smell. "Yeah, it's a goner. Why don't you just order a pizza for dinner instead?"

Donna laughed, the sound filling him with warmth. "Lilly will be thrilled. I feel like a failure, though." Her smile faded.

"Hey." Haven caught her hand and gave it a squeeze. "You're learning. Cooking takes practice. Lilly just appreciates you trying." His thumb stroked over the back of her hand.

A shiver seemed to pass through Donna at his touch. Her eyes lifted to his, a familiar heat simmering in their depths. Haven knew he should drop her hand, step back...but he couldn't seem to make himself break the contact.

The moment was shattered by Lilly bouncing into the kitchen. "Did someone say pizza?" Her eyes landed on their joined hands and widened. A knowing grin spread over her face. Haven dropped Donna's hand as if scalded, clearing his throat. Donna looked away quickly, cheeks flaming. An awkward silence descended, full of unspoken questions and possibilities.

Lilly's grin only grew bigger as she watched them, clearly enjoying their discomfort. "So...about that pizza. Should I call Nicolette for our usual?"

"Please do." Donna turned back to the stove, pushing the pot off the burner. Haven ran a hand through his hair, wondering how he could still want this woman so badly after all they had been through. Wondering if she felt the same. He sighed, pushing the thoughts away. There were too many threats facing them now to act on such feelings. But when this was over - if they made it through in one piece - he knew it was a conversation they could no longer avoid. The sparks between were getting difficult to ignore. He just hoped it didn't end up consuming them both.

Donna looked at him, subtle laughter dancing in her dark eyes. "Nicolette must think I'm a terrible mother. We get pizzas about three times a week. I'm surprised she doesn't just automatically send them up every night."

Haven snorted. "Do you honestly think you're the only ones she cooks for?"

"I know we're not," she said, looking away, "but I want to be able to do more for Lilly."

"Well, you can start with this," he said, handing her the bag.

Donna peered inside. "Two phones?"

"Well, how did you expect to keep track of her?"

Donna looked taken aback, and she blinked. Then she laughed until she had to swipe tears from her eyes. "You know, I was so concentrated on a phone for her I didn't even think about me."

"Now you both have a way to get in touch with each other."

Nodding, she pulled one out of the bag and lifted the lid away. A black, shiny phone was nestled inside, and she smiled sadly. "I haven't had a cell phone for almost five years. Dr. Shu didn't want them in the building for security reasons. He was always afraid someone was going to steal his formula."

"Well, we're trusting you to do what's right. But yours will be monitored as well."

Donna gave him a full smile, and it about bowled Haven over.

"Lilly," she called, "come here."

Lilly bounced into the kitchen, eyes lighting up when she saw the phones. "Are those for us?"

At Donna's nod, she threw her arms around her mother. "Thank you!"

Donna returned the hug fiercely. "You're welcome, sweetheart."

Haven watched them with a smile, warmth blooming in his chest. Donna deserved this joy, this freedom, this chance at a relationship with the daughter she had lost for so long. His eyes met Donna's over Lilly's head, and the depth of emotion he saw in them stole his breath.

Lilly finally released her mom and grabbed one of the phones, immediately customizing settings to her liking. Donna shook her head at the way the girl's fingers flew over the screen. "I have a lot to learn about teenage girls and technology. We're going to have to set some ground rules," she said firmly, but Lilly barely nodded.

"Rules are your domain. I just bring the fun stuff," he laughed. Lilly stopped what she was doing long enough to reach out and give him a fist bump. "But listen. there are some security features on here that you need to know about."

Lilly frowned as she looked at the phone. "Security?"

"Yes, security. Each phone has a GPS tracker in it, of course. It's loaded with every number of every team member, and if you press and hold 1, we know it's an emergency. If you press and hold the volume button, we know it's an emergency."

Lilly blinked, then looked at her mother, her eyes shadowed. "You didn't just give me this out of the kindness of your heart."

"No," Donna agreed, voice subdued. "I know you miss talking to your friends. That's one reason I asked for the phones. But I also need to be able to talk to you. And I need to know where you are at all times."

Lilly's face fell, a little, then she lifted her gaze to her mother. "Do you think the senator is after us again?"

Donna winced. "Well, he's never not been after us, honey. Every time they try the security of the building, they're looking for weaknesses."

Lilly grimaced, and nodded. "Okay. I'll keep it on me as much as I can."

"Good. Now go answer the door. I think Nicolette already had our pizza in the oven."

There was a knock on the door, and Lilly bounced up from the chair to go get it. She returned a few seconds later with a steaming pizza on a platter. Donna looked at Haven. "Will you join us?"

Haven was surprised at the invitation, and he started to smile. Then his own phone went off. He scanned the message. "I'll have to take a raincheck," he murmured.

Lilly had already torn a piece of pizza from the pie and was scrolling on her phone with one hand. She gave him a wave with the pizza as he headed toward the door. Donna followed along behind him, and she seemed to want to say something, so he paused.

"Thank you, Haven," she said simply. Reaching out, she squeezed his forearm, before folding her arms over her stomach again. "I love my daughter, but she's a challenge. I don't always say or do the right things."

"Well, maybe we can figure it out together," Haven said. Donna's smile in return made his heart trip.

Haven hesitated, then reached out to brush a stray hair from Donna's face. Her breath seemed to catch, but she didn't pull away.

"Thank you for this," she said softly. "For giving me a chance...giving us a chance." Her fingers lifted to graze the back of his hand, and Haven shivered. He knew he should step away before he did something reckless. But right now, with her this close, the rest of the world faded away. His thumb traced her cheekbone.

"How could I not?" His voice was rough. Donna's lips parted, eyes clinging to his, and Haven couldn't stop himself from leaning down to steal a taste of the sweetness he had been craving for so long...

When Donna's emotional grid went haywire, Haven jerked back as if stung, cursing under his breath. Donna looked away quickly - but not before he saw a flash of heartache and regret that matched his own. He took a deep, shaky breath, wishing things could be different for them. With a quiet 'goodnight', he let himself out of the apartment.

# 6

Donna let out a very unladylike curse and rested her head on the closed door. That hadn't gone the way she'd wanted it to.

Damn it.

She wasn't an idiot. Haven had been looking at her, thinking about her, the way a man appreciated a woman, and her body had responded. Man, when he'd started in for the kiss, though, her fight or flight brain had kicked in and screwed everything up. Haven was not like the guards the senator had employed. She knew that in her brain and her heart. But she'd been hurt so many times. And abused so many times. It was hard to remember how to have an actual relationship.

She felt like if she could get past this one hurdle, though, her life would be infinitely better. And she would feel more secure. At one time, she'd enjoyed dating and even having sex. She'd fallen in love with her former husband and thought that life couldn't get better. Then she'd gotten pregnant with Lilly, and it had gotten so much sweeter.

Being in the military was hard, though, and when she'd

returned from a deployment overseas, her husband had confessed to having an affair. It had been the beginning of the end for them. The judge had granted him primary custody, and Donna was forced to agree with them. Her lifestyle wasn't ideal for a child, and she still had two years before she could even think about getting out.

A knock at the door behind her made Donna jump. She took a deep breath, steeling herself, and opened it to find Haven on the other side. She thought he'd left.

His expression was serious, cautious, as he glanced behind her. "Can we talk? Out here?"

Donna nodded, then stepped out into the hallway with him. She closed the door softly behind her, hoping that Lilly wouldn't notice she'd gone out. Her pulse raced as Haven leaned against the door-jamb across from her. He ran a hand through his walnut-colored hair, searching for words. "I'm sorry if I overstepped just now. I don't want to pressure you into anything you're not ready for."

"You didn't." Donna took a shaky breath. "I'm just...not very good at this. At trusting that what seems too good to be true possibly might not be."

Haven's expression softened. "I would never hurt you, Donna. But we can go as slowly as you need."

His sincerity made tears sting her eyes. "My life has been a series of loss and betrayal. Abuse. The idea of opening myself up to that again terrifies me." Her voice dropped. "But closing myself off means losing out on joy and connection too. And I'm perilously close to losing myself forever," she admitted.

Haven sighed, and leaned down to look into her eyes. "I understand. It wasn't that long ago when I was lost, and you brought me around. I'll stay close enough to do that for you, but not crowd you. Okay? You are not a lost cause. In the past year

I've seen you open up more than I ever could have hoped, and I'm willing to wait as long as I need to." He gave her a smile. "And Lilly has changed for the better. You two are good for each other."

Donna nodded, fighting tears. This emotion was driving her nuts, but she couldn't seem to control herself around him. "We're good for each other."

"You are," he agreed. Very slowly, giving her time to pull away, he stroked her cheek. Donna turned into his touch, letting him cup her cheek. It felt good, letting him do that. Closing her eyes, she just breathed and felt the emotion. Haven's rough thumb moved back and forth, and she lifted her eyes to his.

"That feels nice. I've... forgotten what it's liked to be touched like that."

"You have the most beautiful skin," he murmured.

Donna choked on a laugh. "For being a vampire, you mean. It seems like forever since I've been out on the sun."

Haven shook his head. "It's beautiful. The paleness suits you."

Donna took his words into her, planting them very carefully in her heart.

"I have to go," he murmured, "but I didn't want to leave you that way before. I wanted you to know it was okay, you pulling away."

Those damn tears were threatening again. "Thank you, Haven."

With a final stroke, he pulled away. Donna watched him walk down the hallway, loose hipped and strong in his dark uniform. Just a year ago he'd been almost at death's door. Turning, she keyed the code and let herself into the apartment.

"If you're done whispering with Haven, the pizza is still warm," Lilly called.

Donna laughed and went to eat pizza with her snarky daughter.

~

LILLY MESSAGED TINI IMMEDIATELY, while her mom was in the hallway with Haven. She wasn't sure why they went out there, but she was going to use the moment to reconnect to her best friend.

The dot icon bounced a few times as her friend read the message and typed out her reply. *NO WAY! FINALLY!*

*Ik, r? I never thought she would. They surprised me with it tonight.*

*They?*

*Yeah, there's this guy, Haven. He's cool. I think he likes my mom. Anyway, he brought them up a few minutes ago.*

*That's so cool! I've missed just picking up the phone and texting you. Oh, I need to send you some pics!*

Lilly waited as a jumble of pictures popped up in a group. *Oh, man, where did you go?*

*Sabrina's mom's place.*

Lilly flicked through the pics of her friends lounging by a pool and shoving hot dogs in their faces. Then she found the one of Asher. It looked like he'd posed for it, muscles flexing in his arms and chest.

*I sent you one of Ash.*

*Yeah, just found it. Sigh...*

*Yeah, I told him it was for you and he totally flexed. Dude has a hard-on for you.*

Lilly's eyes flicked down, even as she felt her cheeks heat. Thank god Mom wasn't in here to feel her reaction. She wasn't sure he had an actual hard-on, but how did she know?

*Well, thanks for the pics. I miss you guys.*

*So, since you got the phone, does that mean you're allowed out?*

*Not hardly. The regime has tightened it's hold. This is merely a pacifier.*

*Well, hell. Can I come down and have lunch with you?*

Lilly stared at the words for a long time. Could Tini come down and have lunch with her? The guys in charge probably wouldn't care, would they? They had bigger fish to fry.

*Maybe. It's a long trip. You sure you want to do that?*

*It's just a train ride down to the city, right?*

*Yeah, I guess.*

*Ok, then I'll do it. I'll be there tomorrow. You'd better meet me!*

*I will*, Lilly typed, then instantly regretted it. Her mom was going to be pissed.

When she returned from the hallway, Lilly told her about reconnecting with Tini, but not about their plans. She was very careful to keep those plans behind a mental wall. It was so hard, because excitement was zinging through her. It had been months since she'd seen anyone, and she was so glad that Tini was coming down. Yes, she'd been a 'prisoner' with the senator's wife, but she'd been able to have a life. She'd gone to school and had friends. She hadn't known where her mother was at the time, so she had been unable to make plans to go see her. Heck, at that time she hadn't even known if her mother was alive or dead. They'd only been able to see each other about twice a year.

Lilly remembered those visits vividly. Every time she'd seen her mother, the woman had looked more and more ragged. More beat down. It had broken her heart to see her that way. So, she'd pretended like everything was okay, and that she wasn't desperately lonely rambling through the big estate, followed by scowling guards. Lilly had lifted her chin and pretended to be stronger than she was.

Man, she'd been lonely. Tini had been the saving grace of being in that damn mausoleum, though. The girl was the same age as Lilly, but only about half her size. People always thought Tini was a child, because of her diminutive stature. She had a personality of a dragon, though, and Lilly loved her to pieces.

Yes, she would meet Tini. Hopefully she could just come here. Maybe she could show her the greenhouse.

Lilly barely slept that night with the anxiety coursing through her. She knew she should talk to her mother. Maybe if she conveyed how important it was to see her school friend, her mom would let her. Surely, she would let her. Lilly drifted off to sleep toward morning, determined to talk to her mom when she got up.

## 7

Their first break came the next morning. Pieter Krammer called them all to his office, in the corner of the first floor. The former German Kommando Spezialkräfte Marine was hunched over his desk, a pair of tweezers in his good right hand as he looked through special glasses at what he held. When they entered the room, he looked up, his eyes magnified by the glasses until he swiped them from his head.

"Ah, *gut*. You must see."

Spinning in his chair, he typed a few commands into the keyboard behind him. The wall display in front of them lit up, and a path of red crisscrossed the city. "This is where the drone has been, while active and not."

Haven walked closer to the display. The lines danced all over the city, but seemed to be concentrated a few miles away from their current location. He pointed at a location a few blocks away. "That was where the un-sub was killed. Where's his base?"

Krammer held up a finger, typing in another command. A single red dot appeared on the map, in an abandoned warehouse district several miles from where the dead man was found. "There. That building has been receiving encrypted signals from the drone for the past several weeks. It seems our ghost was operating from there."

Aiden stepped closer, frowning. "But why lead us to his body? Why reveal that location but hide the base?"

"Misdirection," Haven said grimly. "Whomever is haunting us wanted us chasing clues, while they cleared out that warehouse." He turned to Krammer. "Are they still transmitting from there?"

Krammer shook his head. "The signals went dark shortly after we found the body. I believe they have abandoned the location."

"Then we need eyes on that building now," Aiden said. "Find out if they left anything behind. Haven, get your team together."

Haven sent a mental call to his team, then moved over to the map, eyes tracing the winding path of the drone's signal. His heart had kicked into high gear, the thrill of the hunt singing in his veins. At last, a solid lead—even if their stalker had ultimately slipped away again. He felt Donna step up quietly beside him. He hadn't even noticed when she'd entered the room behind them.

"We're getting close," she murmured.

Haven glanced at her. Her eyes were fixed on the map, expression unreadable. "Have you been there before?" he asked gently. "The warehouse district?"

Donna shook her head. "But any place this operative has been is somewhere I need to be." She finally looked at him. "I'm going with you."

"I don't think that's a good idea." Haven planted his feet and shook his head. "You are one of the assets they want. It would be stupid to take you outside these walls."

"I'm going, Haven. I need to know who it is. I'm pretty sure it's McCullough, and if it is, I have a score to settle. I'll be able to read the place better than all of you will."

Haven opened his mouth to protest but quickly shut it again. He knew better by now than to argue with Donna once her mind was made up. And she deserved to be there to witness the aftermath as much as any of them. "All right," he conceded. "Just..." he shook his head again, mouth working. She was very aware that her going with them would amp up the danger, but she felt like she needed to be there. "Go change," he said, finally, voice resigned.

With a nod, Donna left the room to get ready. Haven stared at the empty doorway and tried to ignore Krammer's curious gaze. His chest felt suddenly tight, dread and adrenaline mingling as the threat they were facing loomed larger than ever. Donna tagging along was not in the plans, but he would protect her with his life.

DONNA DIDN'T second guess what she was doing as she changed out of her sweater and slacks into dark jeans and a dark long-sleeved shirt. She pulled a heavy-duty windbreaker over everything. She would ask for a weapon of some kind. It was early, and Lilly was still sleeping, so she left her a note on the table where it would be seen. Then she headed back down to the office. Her heart was racing at the thought of getting out of the building, even if it was on a wild goose chase.

When she ducked her head into Krammer's office, Haven was gone. "Parking garage," the German told her.

Donna hustled down the hallway, nodding at the guards stationed at the elevator. When they saw her coming, one of them reached back and pressed the call button. Donna didn't remember his name, but she smiled a thank you, which seemed to surprise him. Was she really that dour that a smile surprised a man? Apparently.

Haven and his team were waiting at the elevator landing for her. Before she could even open her mouth, Haven was handing her a pistol in a pancake holster. "It's chambered, but the safety is on. I know you carried a Beretta M9 in the Army. This is the closest thing we had."

Quickly and efficiently, Donna slid the Sig Sauer from the holster and checked it. "This is fine. I've shot one of these before."

"Okay. Let's go."

They walked her to one of the black Suburbans. There was a second Suburban just pulling out. "That's team two. Perkins, Slack, Abioye, and Manchester."

Donna nodded, appreciating the intel. She opened her senses and felt the men inside the first truck. She recognized them all, though she doubted she could name them all. One man, Slack, she'd helped before. She recognized his energy signature. She couldn't remember exactly what she'd done for him, but maybe when she saw him she would remember. Not that it was especially important right now.

Copper climbed into the driver's seat, Haven riding shotgun. That left her to sit between Dex and Jibari. It was fine, though. She knew they were on business and had no qualms about touching them in this way.

"Team two will set up a perimeter and we'll let Dex out to get a sniff of the place. See who's pissed on the fire hydrants."

Haven flicked a smiling look back at her, and she snorted.

"Really," Dex said, voice wry. "Dog jokes? Haven't heard that before."

Copper drove like a man on a mission, and Donna almost laughed. His driving would fit in with all the other government black Suburbans floating around the area. It was a clever camouflage. Within a few minutes, they were pulling into an industrial area. Haven checked his phone and motioned forward. "One block down and one to the east, and we'll park."

The warehouse loomed before them, a crumbling relic from an industrial era long past. Copper parked a safe distance away, and Haven's team filed out of their vehicles, weapons at the ready. Donna slid out behind Dex, her borrowed pistol a comforting weight in her hands. Adrenaline sang through her veins at the prospect of finally gaining some insight into who was hunting them. She inhaled deeply, filtering through the scents around them for any clue the normal senses might miss. It was bitterly cold this morning, and their breath misted the air.

Dex tilted his head, nostrils flaring as he sorted through the olfactory clues for recent activity. "There's the smell of diesel and motor oil, old and dried out. But underneath that..." His brow furrowed. "I'm picking up traces of C4 and gunpowder. And blood. Whoever was here, they were armed and things got violent."

Haven's jaw tightened, eyes scanning the building. "Explosives. Just what we need. Everyone proceed with caution, check for tripwires or pressure plates. And be on guard for any nasty surprises left behind."

The teams broke off to circle the warehouse, searching for the best way inside. Haven turned to Donna, expression grim. "I want you staying with me or Dex at all times. No wandering off."

She nodded, swallowing down a flare of indignation. His protectiveness was endearing, even if it chafed. And his worry was not misplaced. Who knew what dangers lurked within these walls, or if the former resident might return.

Dex paused before a side entrance, head cocked. "Here. I smell blood and gunpowder strongest by this door. I think our tango entered and exited here." Haven signaled the teams, and they converged by the doorway.

"Proceed with extreme caution. Dex, you take point with Donna and I. Check for traps every step of the way."

Dex eased the door open with gloved hands, surveying the area before waving them inside. The interior was musty and dim, shafts of light piercing through holes in the roof to spot the concrete floor below. Dust motes swirled in the stale air, clinging to discarded machinery and industrial debris.

Donna peered into the gloom, heart pounding as she strained all her senses for some hint of the threat that lurked at the edges of their lives. She could feel the residue of violence here, echoes of panic and aggression that lingered like a miasma. Their adversary had come and gone, but left darkness in their wake. Slowly they crept deeper into the warehouse.

Donna opened her senses wide, feeling for any kind of life. The building seemed dead. Derelict. A shiver chased down her spine, and she moved closer to Haven's back. Something about this place was... haunting.

As soon as Lilly found the note on the table, she knew she'd missed her chance. She should have talked to her mother last night and cleared things. Now she would have to beg forgiveness rather than permission.

Tini messaged her when she was on the train. And an hour later when she got to the train station.

*Drop me a pin so I know where you are. So, should I just go to the front door?*

Lilly had been struggling with this, and she thought she'd come up with a solution. *No, come to the loading dock around back. Stop and pick up some kind of delivery bag, Starbucks or something.*

*Okay, I'll meet you there in ten minutes.*

Tini sent her a thumbs up.

Lilly went down to the kitchen. All of the guards she saw, she told them where she was going, and they all nodded. Apparently, they didn't think she could get into any trouble as long as she stayed within the building. And she planned to stay within the building. They had an access point for deliveries, though. It was only two guards, and she'd waited with them for deliveries before. She had a feeling she could sweet-talk them into letting Tini through.

The kitchen was surprisingly quiet when she entered. Nicolette was nowhere to be seen, which was strange. She was always in the kitchen. Oh, maybe she was short-handed again and delivering a meal. Lilly knew it had been hard for Nic to find people to work with. For a while, the head chef had been working with a couple of the rehabilitated men, but maybe they had grown out of the position. More often than not, it was just Nic down here, cooking her ass off. Lilly had been down several times on snack runs, and sometimes Nic let her help cook a meal. She especially loved baking the cookies, and getting them just perfect.

Helping Nic was another reason she'd chosen for Tini to come here. The guards knew her, and they knew she helped out down here a good bit.

She glanced at the phone clock. It had been twelve minutes since she'd talked to Tini. Was she stuck in line somewhere? Where the heck was she?

～

ROGER MCCULLOUGH COULDN'T BELIEVE his luck. Two of the teams were out of the Elton Recovery building at once. He also knew that a third was on a training exercise. Did he go after the primary target, heading down the street in one of the Suburbans, or did he go after the secondary target? Either would be dangerous, but he knew the two teams that had left were probably the strongest in the building. He hadn't seen Wulfe Terberger or Aiden Willingham in either of the vehicles, though. So, face the two big dogs in the building with a handful of lame ducks, or eight strong operatives in the Suburbans? He would love to get his hands on the baby, but he'd lost his chance to do that in Colorado. She would be too well-guarded here.

There was a security notification on his phone and he scrolled through the feed. The fuckers were in his warehouse. His hideout. He'd expected them to find it, but it still burned. Now he was even more glad he'd killed Kelley, because obviously they'd gotten the geo-location off the damned drone. Fuck. Well, what else did he have to lose, then? He would force his way in and pray he found the kid. He didn't think he was strong enough mentally to take on the German or Willingham, but he would go up against them physically any time of day.

Or maybe he would take one of the females. Dr. Elizabeth Cole would be an excellent grab.

Who was he kidding? There was no way he'd be able to make it through the building without being seen or felt, and there were men inside who had abilities he knew nothing about. He was sure of it. It had been a long time since Dr. Cole's assistant had defected with that list of names and sold it to the senator. By now, he knew the number of residents had at least doubled, and there were men in training now that could probably kick his ass.

Choices, choices...

Someone must have been looking out for him. At that moment, two kids passed by, and he caught a snippet of conversation. 'Lilly is such a great girl. Though her living situation is a little strange.'

The teenage boy with her said something in a laughing voice, and continued to saunter down the street without a care in the world. A Starbucks bag swung from the short girl's left hand, while the right paged through apps on her phone, even as she continued to talk. The boy carried a drink carrier with three cups, but he was slurping on the straw of one. Neither one noticed him fall in behind them.

What were the fucking chances? Someone was looking out for him.

If these two were on their way to meet Lilly, maybe he could draw her out instead. He needed to move quickly if he was going to, though.

Camouflaging himself in a gray shroud to match the building shadows, he caught up with the kids. One well-placed strike took the teenage boy out. Sugary coffee treats spilled on the ground as the cups smashed down. He grabbed the boy under the arms and set him aside before the girl even realized her companion was out of commission. Mentally, he shook his head at the stupidity of the young.

Before the girl could scream when she saw her friend, he wrapped an arm around her head. "One sound and I will literally break your neck."

He flexed his arm and cut off her air supply for emphasis, then decided that was a good idea anyway. With just a little prolonged pressure, he knocked the girl out. Then he dragged them both behind some shrubs. The girl's phone was still clutched in her hand. Peeling her fingers away, he scrolled through the text messages. Yes, there it was.

*Lilly,* he typed out. *If you want to see your friends again, you need to come out and get them.* For added threat, he snapped a picture of the two laying on the ground, and sent it along with the message.

Almost immediately, a response came through. *Give me time to get around security.*

Roger grinned, and glanced around to make sure no one had noticed them. The street was fairly quiet, and the kids were hidden well enough. Merging back into the shadows, he waited for his prey to come to him.

When he'd gone rogue, his options had vaporized. He was on the run, now, and he knew the Secret Service was actively looking for him. He was one of the few that had escaped capture and prosecution with the senator, and he planned to secure his own future before he disappeared completely. He had a bunker in Oklahoma with his name on it, as well as a new identity.

If he could get Lilly, or her mother Belladonna, he would make Pike pay out the ass for them. He knew the punk kid had access to the senator's coffers, and he wanted his share. The senator had cost him his career and life, and he would be paying one way or the other.

Roger waited in the shadows, anticipation building as the minutes ticked by. His trap was set, the bait laying helpless on the ground behind him. All that remained was for the prey to arrive. He checked his watch, impatience growing as twenty minutes passed with no sign of the girl. Were the security measures around her too great to evade? Were they even now planning a counterattack? His hands tightened into fists at his side, mind racing through contingencies. He would not leave here empty handed, damn it.

Just as his flight instinct almost took hold, a slender figure in a dark jacket crept around the corner of the building ahead of him. The girl glanced around furtively before rushing over to where her friends lay. Roger dropped his camouflage, wrapped an arm around her throat and pressed the gun to her head. "Hello, Lilly. Long time no see. Make a sound, and you'll be celebrating your last birthday. Do you understand?"

The girl whimpered, frozen in terror. Her thin body trembled in his grasp. "Please," she whispered. "Don't hurt them. I'll do whatever you want."

Roger grinned. His prize was won. "Smart girl. Your friends will live - as long as you cooperate. Give me your phone." As soon as she handed it over, he zip-tied her wrists and shoved her down the alley and into the van he'd stolen this morning. It was beige and nondescript, which suited his needs perfectly.

His leverage was secured. As the van roared down the road, Roger glanced back at the girl. She was sobbing quietly in the rear of the van, clutching her legs and rocking. Completely broken. A flare of disappointment went through him. He had snatched the girl hoping for a stronger target and found only a helpless victim. She held no value to him, merely as a bargaining chip. The mother was the one he wanted. Taking the child had been a coup, and he wondered how long it would take Belladonna to realize.

She would come for her child. And he would be ready for her.

## 8

The warehouse was a maze of booby traps and hideaways, and it had Roger McCullough's prints all over it, metaphorically speaking. The former Secret Service agent, appointed by the president, had guarded Senator Hall. According to Wulfe, it had seemed like he was the number one when it came to security. Supposedly he was working for the government, but Hall had corrupted McCullough. They had researched him for months, digging into his background and they'd found the exact point when Hall had swayed him. McCullough's sister had been killed in a car crash. Deliberately or accidentally, they couldn't tell for sure. They wouldn't put it past Hall to take out family to attain his goal, if he was actively recruiting McCullough. She'd been his only living relative, and soon after that they believe he'd been dosed with a Marathon serum derivative. Elizabeth had found a single reference to the agent, and that he'd responded better to MI4-3 than the other four who had been given the same drug.

Haven didn't know if Agent McCullough understood what he was getting into when he allowed himself to be a guinea pig, but it was neither here nor there now. The guy had turned dirty and taken the drug, and he'd been on the lamb stalking them for the better part of the last year. Noah and Raine had followed Haven to New York in search of Belladonna thirteen months ago. That was the last time McCullough had been seen in public.

They weren't sure what abilities the drug had given him, but Haven had a feeling it was camouflage similar to what he could do. The guy was a shadow, unseen in the night. In Colorado he'd had people he was working with, but it was obvious by the body they found yesterday that he didn't get attached.

Haven looked around the building. There was evidence of several people staying here, but it may have just been the dead body they'd found yesterday and McCullough.

"How many scents are you picking up, Dex?"

"Half a dozen, easy. Though a couple are older. Like, more than a week. Two are very distinctive."

"Roger that," he murmured, shining a flashlight up into the rafters. His light flashed on something. "We've got eyes," he murmured. Keying the mic he wore, he contacted Krammer. "Can you figure out if these feeds are live?"

The tech murmured on the other end. "Give me a moment." There was clattering on the other end, like he was working his keyboard. "Yes, I believe so. Let me see..."

Haven shined the light all along the ceiling, looking for more. Seemed like there was only the one. In this room, at least.

"I'm patched in," Krammer murmured. "Now let me see where this goes. It feeds to a mobile..."

Donna staggered and clutched his arm, swaying. She drew in a gasping breath. "Haven, something's wrong. We need to get back to the Elton building."

Haven looked at her. Fear was etched in her face, and her eyes were wide open. "What's wrong?"

She shook her head and winced, like she was trying to reach for something.

"Team leader," Krammer interrupted, "that mobile is outside our building and moving south."

"Team Two, back to the car, now!"

Haven turned Donna and they took off running. They'd cleared most of the traps they'd found, so it was easier going out than coming in, but they still proceeded with caution. They burst into the alley as a group and bolted for the car. Copper was pulling away before Dex had even closed the door as he scrambled in behind her.

"Talk to me, Krammer."

"I'm looking through the feeds now. It, it appears that Ms. Lilly left the building."

Donna voiced an inarticulate cry and Haven reached a hand back to her. Her emotional grid was going haywire. "We don't know what she was doing. Let's just give him a minute."

Haven's jaw tightened as Krammer relayed the news. Lilly had slipped past security in the delivery bay and out of the Elton building. The implications rocked through him, and he glanced back at Donna.

"Do we have eyes on her now?" His voice was steady, belying the tension thrumming through every limb. Behind him, Donna clutched his hand with white knuckles, face pale. He knew this was her ultimate fear.

"Negative. I've accessed traffic cameras along possible routes from the building but there's no sign of her yet." Krammer typed furiously, much faster than a one-handed typist should have been able to. "She must have taken side streets to avoid major surveillance points."

Donna made a low, wounded sound. Haven squeezed her hand gently. "We'll find her. She couldn't have gotten far."

"Here! Three blocks west of Elton. I've got a visual." Krammer magnified the footage, cursing under his breath. The image was dark, grainy, but the sight of a familiar figure being shoved into a van was unmistakable. Their enemy had attacked when they were most vulnerable. As quickly as Lilly appeared, she vanished from view. The van had pulled away, taillights fading into the night. Haven heard Krammer slam a fist onto the desk. "I'm sorry, I lost the vehicle. No clear shot of a plate. The only identifiable mark on it was a taillight was out. Passenger side." His voice was thick with frustration and guilt. "I should have caught this sooner."

"What's done is done," Haven said, drawing a deep breath. "We need to mobilize and get search efforts underway now." Haven fought to keep his tone steady and sure. There was no time for recriminations or wasted effort. Action and a clear head were needed. Donna lifted her gaze to meet his, dark pupils dilated with fear. But under the fear was iron will and determination. Somehow, she'd managed to drag her emotions back under control. She gave a short, sharp nod. Haven turned to the team, spine rigid with purpose. "We have a child to recover. All hands on deck - sweep the city, check anywhere they could possibly hide. Leave no stone unturned." The team voiced their agreement, mobilizing into a well-oiled machine. In minutes, Copper was cruising the area where Lilly had been taken.

"Let me out," Dex said.

"I want out, too," Donna murmured, sliding out after him.

Cursing, Haven slid out as well, glancing at Jibari and Copper. "Circle the block, then work your way out."

Copper pulled away with a nod, the Suburban revving. As Haven followed Dex and Donna, he called Wulfe and recapped the past forty minutes. Wulfe cursed and began typing on his computer, probably pulling up the feed

Krammer had flagged. "That's definitely McCullough. Son of a bitch! Let me make some calls."

Haven didn't know who he was going to call, but he let him go. They'd reached the corner where Lilly had been taken. Donna headed toward a copse of overgrown bushes. "Here!" she called out.

They found two teenage kids unconscious on the ground, but unharmed for the most part. Donna turned the girl's face up. "This is Lilly's friend Tini, I think."

Donna closed her eyes and rested her hand on the girl's forehead. It was easy to see the last few minutes of what they had been doing. "They were coming to meet Lilly. She didn't see the man who grabbed her."

Haven gave her a long look. "Wulfe confirmed it was McCullough."

Donna's face closed down, her lips tightening with fury. "I'm going to kill him. Just get me close, Haven."

Haven nodded, resting a hand on her shoulder. "I'll do what I can," he promised.

That seemed to be enough for her. They called a squad for the kids, then made them as comfortable as possible. Then they began walking the area in a grid. Dex had found where McCullough had loaded Lilly into the van. It was an alley hidden from any type of surveillance.

"He knows we'll be coming for him," Donna murmured, her anxiety building again, "but he's going to call. He's going to want to do a swap, for me. And, knowing McCullough, he's going to take us both, because she's the perfect leverage to keep me in line. They've proven that. It worked for them for years."

Haven stopped Donna with hands on her shoulders. She was crying, but he didn't even think she realized it. He wiped her face with his thumbs. "Hey, you need to stop. We're going to find her. McCullough seems to be working alone, and we just crashed his hangout, so he's running scared."

"He probably has a backup spot," she said quietly, blinking the tears from her eyes.

"I agree. Let's go back to the Dog Pound and we'll see if we can squeeze more info out of that drone. Or maybe we'll squeeze it out of Krammer." He gave her a teasing smile, and she responded for a moment, nodding.

"Let's go."

## 9

L illy continued to sniffle, though the actual tears had dried up a while ago. Now she was just mad. This asshole had hurt her friends, and they would never come see her again. And when she got back, her mom was going to literally lock her in her room and throw away the key.

Damn it.

She'd known what she was doing was wrong, and now she was paying for it.

Mom was going to be livid. And scared. Lilly felt real tears start in her eyes as she thought about her mother's reaction. They'd only just gotten back on even footing. Though she hadn't lived with her mother full-time for a long time because of her military career, the past year had been a lot of fun, getting to know her again. She still missed her dad, but Mom held a very special spot in her life. Lilly knew her mother struggled with a lot of things, but she felt like she'd helped her over the past year. They'd helped each other.

She sniffled again, trying not to over-act. If the McCullough asshole viewed her as a weak female, all the better. Maybe he wouldn't notice what she'd done.

The weight of her phone in her sock felt conspicuous, and she forced her hands not to go there to hide the item. McCullough had patted her down lightly, but he apparently didn't think she was smart enough to hide anything on herself. Or maybe he was just too cocky. Once they stopped, she would key the volume button. That would have the Dogs of War running to find her. And if her mother got her hands on this guy, he was going to die a horrible death.

Maybe he needed reminded of that fact.

Lilly lifted her head and watched the back of Roger's head. "You know my mother is going to kill you when she gets her hands on you."

He turned to face her slightly, smirking. "She's never going to get her hands on me. I'm going to get my hands on her," he stressed. "Your mother needs her collar on."

Fury flowed through Lilly, and it took everything she had to stay seated in the seat. "You're an asshole."

"Yup, I am. And I'm a broke asshole. Your mother, and maybe even you for that matter, are the payday I've been waiting for. So sit back and shut up before I gag you."

Lilly decided to do what he said, just because she didn't want anything from this car in her mouth. It looked like five little kids had raided a candy store and left the remnants behind. Or maybe the mother that drove this piece of shit had raided the store to feed her little beasties. It was disgusting in here.

Sinking back in the seat, she watched out the window. She didn't recognize where they were and he had probably planned it that way. It would make her less likely to escape.

Suddenly she felt very alone. She didn't want to have anything to do with this guy, or the people they hung around with. The senator was in prison, but that didn't mean he didn't still have business going on outside. Obviously, he had someone looking out for his interests. Or maybe their interests, since the senator was in jail. She was sure he was still pulling the strings, though.

For a moment, hopelessness overwhelmed her, and her eyes filled with tears. She refused to give Roger the satisfaction of seeing her cry again, though.

∾

HAVEN DIDN'T LIKE the way Donna was acting. He could see her withdrawal with his very eyes. He had a feeling she was already preparing herself to be a prisoner again. "Donna," he murmured.

She blinked and glanced at him. Her arms were crossed protectively over her stomach, like she was waiting for a punch. She stared at the screens in front of her sightlessly. "Yes."

Haven took her arm in his hand and drew her out of the tech room. Then he guided her down the hallway to one of the empty offices. Closing the door behind them, he leaned his back against it. "Talk to me. Tell me what you're thinking."

Donna shook her head. "You don't want to know."

"I think I have some idea. You're thinking you would happily swap yourself for Lilly."

"I would," she said immediately, her dark eyes blazing with determination.

Haven shook his head, frustrated. "You know he's not going to release her. He's going to use her as leverage against you."

Donna winced and looked at her feet. "Perhaps," she admitted softly.

"We can not allow him to get his hands on you," Haven said sternly. "You're too valuable."

Donna gave him a withering look. "I don't care what I'm worth. I care what my daughter is worth, and I would give myself over in a heartbeat if it meant she could come home."

"I know you would," Haven said softly, stepping toward her. "I know you didn't get to have the kind of relationship you wanted with her, and you feel like you owe her for that. But know this. Lilly would not want you to be back in their hands. I can guarantee that."

Donna shook her head, glancing toward the door. "I'm sure she never actually expected to be kidnapped. Kids never think of that stuff."

"Lilly was aware of her situation," he said quietly.

Donna studied Haven's face, and she must have seen the sincerity and concern he had for them both. He stepped closer, taking her hands in his. "Lilly knew the dangers that could exist for her and for you. But she chose to build a relationship with you anyway. She loves you, and the last thing she would want is for you to sacrifice yourself on her behalf."

Donna glanced away, eyes glistening. "I've already sacrificed so much time with her. I can't lose her now. Not when we've just found each other again." Her voice broke on the last words.

Haven squeezed her hands gently. "You won't. We are going to get her back, together and without handing over the advantage to McCullough. Your daughter is strong, resourceful - she will survive until we find her. Have faith in that."

Donna took a shuddering breath, then met his gaze once more. Her eyes held a gleam of determination now, the makings of a plan. "You said Lilly knew the dangers. Does that mean she may have...prepared somehow? A way to call for help or throw them off guard?"

Haven gave a grim smile. "Your daughter is very clever, and we haven't found her phone. If anything can lead us to her or give us an advantage, Lilly would have found a way."

Donna matched his smile with one of her own. They had a direction now, a source of hope to chase. Her shoulders straightened, confidence returning in the face of action. "Then let's get started. The sooner we pick up the trail, the less time he has with her. I want my little girl back, and McCullough is going to regret this day."

She strode from the room with new purpose, determination in every step. Haven followed after, pride blossoming in his chest. The fighter's spirit he so admired was awakening, and woe be to any who stood in this mother's way. McCullough had no concept of the wrath he would face for taking her child. But he would learn soon enough.

When they returned to the office, Krammer had news. "Her phone is on her, I believe, but I think he has something jamming the signal. I can ping her phone in the alley where you found her friends, but it's not there now. So it must be with her. Or damaged and in a corner somewhere."

Haven shook his head. "No, I think Dex would have scented it. There was nothing else around there."

Krammer shrugged. "Maybe he tossed it out the window."

They stood in there, crowding the tech room for almost an hour, when he got a call from Copper. "Yeah, Cop. What's up?"

"I just caught a glimpse of a van that looked like the one we were looking for entering a parking garage in DC. He may be looking to swap out vehicles."

"Where?"

"Corner of E Street and Massachusetts Ave. It's a tourist garage."

Krammer called the map up on the screens and narrowed in on the location. "Can you get close enough to ID him?"

Copper huffed out a breath, and it sounded like he was jogging. "Gonna try." They listened to him huff through the garage, big feet pounding on the concrete. Then everything went quiet. "He's switching to a white Toyota Camry, four door. Blacked out windows. I can't see Lilly, but I assume she's in there already."

There was a rustling, and a curse. "I only caught a partial Pennsylvania plate. Charles Victor Xray. I couldn't see the numbers."

Krammer was typing away on the keyboard. "I have a lot of options for the letters. I'll start going through them."

They heard Copper running again. "I don't know if I'll make it to the car in time to catch them."

Krammer pounded on the keyboard, spinning in his chair. "I'll keep watch with the DC CCTV until you catch up."

Haven didn't want to know if they even had permission to do that.

Tension coiled through the room as Krammer cycled through camera feeds, searching for any sign of the vehicle. Seconds ticked by with agonizing slowness, each one taking Lilly further from their grasp.

Haven squeezed Donna's shoulder in silent support. She covered his hand with her own, and surprisingly, she leaned into his side. Their shared warmth and proximity seemed to help ground her amidst the swirl of fear and anticipation.

Raised voices suddenly erupted from the speaker, echoing harshly in the concrete garage. Krammer gave a shout of triumph, mobilizing all screens onto a single camera feed. The white Camry was stalled behind another vehicle, turn signal blinking to exit the garage. But a familiar hulking form blocked its way - Copper had caught up to them at last. His gun was drawn and aimed at the driver's side window. "Out of the vehicle now, McCullough! Hands where I can see them."

The window rolled down with excruciating slowness. But the face that emerged was not McCullough's. An old woman glanced fearfully between Copper and the gun trained on her, hands visibly shaking as she raised them. "Please don't shoot! I'm just an Uber driver. I don't know anything about a McCullough!"

Her panicked voice echoed in the confined space. Copper did not lower his weapon. "Where is your passenger?"

"I don't have one." The woman was crying now, terrified of the stranger accosting her with a gun. "I'm between fares. Please..."

Haven closed his eyes, cursing under his breath. Another dead end, and their foe remained one step ahead. How had McCullough discovered their attempt to track him via CCTV? Did he know Copper was running him down? Obviously, he supposed.

McCullough was cunning, but this spoke of planning. There seemed no other way he could have evaded them so thoroughly. Donna's expression was bleak as she turned into Haven's embrace. Not looking a gift horse in the mouth, he wrapped his arms around her shoulders, feeling them quiver. He would fix this for her in a nanosecond of he could. After a moment she stepped back, eyes hardened to flint.

"Get me everything we know about that garage. Staff schedules, camera access logs, client lists. McCullough had help there and someone is going to pay for obstructing us." Her words were edged with violence barely restrained. "No one takes my child and lives to profit from it."

The tiger had emerged in truth now, claws bared and ready to rend anything in her path.

∿

THE CO-CONSPIRATOR WAS a little old woman with a bowl cut of thick, gray hair. She struck Haven as a retired school-teacher, and he wondered where her retired, fisherman husband was. She was just so... ordinary. There was a gleam in her eye, though, that told him everything was going to be a fight.

Copper had pulled the woman from her car, not worrying that the vehicle now blocked several lanes of traffic. This was more important. He'd sequestered her in a parking garage office, a few feet away.

Copper stood, arms crossed, in front of the door and refused to let her leave. When he informed her they they were part of the CIA, she seemed to wilt a little, but rebounded quickly. "I want a lawyer!"

Haven glanced at Copper. *Has she been like this the entire time?*

It had taken them the better part of an hour to get here across the river from Alexandria, with the backed up traffic around the Mall. There was a team upstairs processing the tan van, and Aiden had told Haven to question the suspect. Now, Donna stood beside him, glaring at the driver. Haven held her hand in a death-grip, just to keep her from lashing out at the sexagenarian. Or maybe she was a septuagenarian. Haven wasn't good at guessing ages, but the woman had to be late sixties, early seventies. Set in her ways and knowing she was right in everything.

When she looked at Donna, though, something wavered in her eyes. Like she could see her death coming.

Haven glanced down. Donna's face had closed down, and there was a remote, withdrawn expression in her eyes. Within mere seconds, she'd turned into Belladonna. His gut quivered at the look on her cold face, and for a heartbeat in time, the fear of that moment when she'd rested her hand on his head swept through him. Very negligently, she had cast him aside, and he remembered the pain that followed. Months of torture and neglect, starvation.

Lifting his head, he took a breath, tamping those memories down. That was years in his past, now, and she wasn't what he'd thought she was. She wasn't the bogeyman that Dr. Shu had made her out to be. She was just a woman in an untenable position, doing the best she could for her daughter.

That fierceness was epic, though, and her attention was on the senior citizen in front of her.

Before she could let loose, Haven leaned down to look into her eyes. She refused to look at him, until he turned her head toward him. Reluctantly, her gaze met his. "I know what you're thinking," he murmured, "but you have to take care. In the state you're in you'll kill her."

He felt the flare of terror from the old woman, and she pushed back in the office chair.

Donna must have felt it too, because she glanced at the woman, mouth clenched. "If she doesn't tell me what I want to know, I will strip her mind."

There was another flare of terror, and Haven turned to the old woman. "Ma'am, we're on the trail of a murderer and kidnapper. I need you to tell us what exactly happened in this garage today. What's your name?"

"Rosemary Louden," the woman said, folding her hands across her lap. "I don't appreciate the way I've been treated."

"Have you been hurt in any way?" Haven asked.

"Well, no, but..."

"As I said, we're investigating a man who murdered an accomplice yesterday and kidnapped a young girl today. Do you know anything about that?"

Mrs. Louden started to shake her head, then she frowned. "There was a young girl?"

"Yes, ma'am," Haven said. "She's almost seventeen years old."

Haven let the information settle on her, and he could see the woman's demeanor soften. "I didn't see the girl, but I've driven for Roger a couple of times. He always tips well, because I let him pay with cash. I had to take a second job because the school is trying to move me along, but I'm not ready to go yet."

Haven nodded, encouraging her to talk. "You usually have to have a card?"

Mrs. Louden nodded, eyes flicking back and forth between them. "Yes, but I know he's had issues getting a job as well."

Haven didn't say anything, just gave her an open expression, encouraging her to talk. "Roger said he was protecting the girl from a stalker and getting her out of town as quickly as he could."

Haven glanced at Donna. Her face had chilled, and Mrs. Louden seemed to sense that something was brewing. "I don't question every customer that steps through the door. If I did, I'd never get anything done."

"Did they say where they were going?"

She shook her head, mouth tight, and he wondered if she did know something. Donna seemed to think so too, because she reached out a hand. Mrs. Louden shrank back from her touch, but Belladonna took a long step forward and rested her palm on the woman's forehead. Mrs. Louden slumped in her chair.

"What did he talk about," she said softly.

Mrs. Louden blinked, her gaze hazy, unfocused. "He didn't talk to me, but he told the girl to behave or he would break her neck. She kind of fell getting in the car, and he jerked on her arm. It was obvious it hurt, but the girl didn't say a thing."

A snarl curled Donna's mouth, and she pressed harder on the woman's head. "What... did... he... say?"

Mrs. Louden's skin paled, and her eyes fluttered. "He said they needed to get out of town before they found them, but that he needed to make a stop. He said something about 'the asshole', but he didn't say where he was going. I swear! I just drove him around the parking garage for a few minutes until he pointed at a truck. I stopped, he paid me and they got out."

Belladonna scanned the woman's mind, but was very careful to leave it intact. She filtered through five million little details, and focused in on the day. McCullough had dragged Lilly by the arm, and the girl had tripped as she'd gotten in the car. The vision was a little weird because it was reversed from Mrs. Louden looking in the mirror as they got into her back seat. McCullough was icy cold, his lean face looking even leaner than it had a year ago. It was obvious being on the run didn't suit him. The thin beard he'd worn had thickened, like he didn't take the time to shave regularly. Or maybe he hoped it was different enough from his Secret Service persona that no one would look at him. Whatever the reason, he looked unkempt.

Lilly seemed fine, though. There as no blood or bruising on her, that she could see. Her eyes were clear, and she scanned the area as he hauled her around by the arm.

Good girl. Stay aware.

McCullough hauled her into the cab of a black F150, and Donna shook her head. One of the most ubiquitous vehicles in the world. Had Mrs. Loudon looked down? Oh, she had. It was backwards, but she could puzzle out the plate.

She did one more passthrough of Mrs. Louden's mind, then released her. The old woman slumped in the chair.

Haven leaned down to catch her eye, and Donna gave him a nod. "I'm okay. I've got the info." She looked back at the dazed-eyed woman. "You need to pay more attention to your husband. And I don't mean bitch at him about everything under the sun. You are a very hard woman to love."

Tear's filled Mrs. Louden's eyes, and she looked away. They didn't say anything else as they left the office. "Do you have paper and a pen?"

"No, but you have a notes app on your phone."

Donna retrieved the phone from her pocket and let Haven show her what he meant. Using the tiny pen, she wrote down the letters from the license plate. "It's a Virginia plate. Driver's side panel has some damage."

Haven called it in and set Krammer looking for the vehicle.

Copper was waiting outside, and he stepped in front of Donna. "I'm sorry," he said simply.

Sighing, she shook her head. "It wasn't your fault. I know you did what you could."

Copper fell into step beside them as they exited the garage, still clearly troubled. "I should have secured the area better. He slipped right past me...again."

Donna stopped, turning to face him fully. "Don't blame yourself. McCullough has evaded capture from the best for years - your team found more leads today than any have before." Her voice softened. "We will get him."

Copper studied her for a long moment, then gave a slow nod. Some of the tension eased from his hunched frame at her reassurance. For all his formidable size and skills, he was still just a man seeking redemption and approval.

Haven squeezed Donna's hand gently, acknowledging her kindness. She was learning to inspire loyalty through compassion rather than fear. He was proud to see the wary bonds of trust forming between her and his squad.

His phone buzzed, Krammer on the other end. "We got a

hit on that plate from a traffic cam 30 minutes west of you. Sending coordinates now."

Donna was already jogging toward their vehicle, focused entirely on the hunt.

The coordinates led them back across the river to a derelict barn off a barely-there dirt road. Tire tracks in the thick dust were the only signs of recent activity. Moving with stealth born of experience, they surrounded the structure and breached from multiple points. But the interior was empty, save for the abandoned black F150, a pile of ropes and trash in one stall and skid marks leading out the large bay doors at the rear. McCullough had slipped free again, leaving behind only echoes of what might have been. They had no idea what kind of car he was in now.

Donna knelt to examine the ropes, expression grim. With each dead end, her fears grew that time was running out. Haven shared a look with Dex. They could all feel her radiating pain. Stepping close, he rested a hand on her shoulder. She leaned briefly into his warmth. When she rose to address the team, her spine was steel but her eyes remained bleak. "We have a new trail to follow. I want all available intel on where those tracks may lead, no matter how small it seems. Somewhere out there is our path forward."

The team mobilized swiftly, well attuned now to both the drive and quiet desperation that had sharpened their leader's focus. Each setback only narrowed her world further to bringing Lilly home. For all their skills and determination, would they be able to succeed?

Copper fell into step beside Haven as they left the barn, his expression troubled. "We're running out of time. She won't stop, even if we ask it of her."

Haven watched as Donna slipped into the passenger seat, exhaustion etched in every line yet still relentless hope burned. "No, she won't. But there may be another way."

An idea had begun to take form, a dangerous gambit but perhaps their only chance left. He slid into the driver's seat and took Donna's hand. She glanced up as he gave it a squeeze, puzzled at his smile.

"I think I know how we can draw him out. But you have to trust me, no matter what."

# 10

When they headed for a roadside motel, Donna almost choked on her fear. They couldn't give up on finding Lilly.

Haven must have sensed her panic, because he turned in his seat to face her. "We're not giving up on finding her, but we are going to stop chasing them. The more we chase the more he runs, and we need him to stop running and feel secure. Then he'll call us for ransom."

What he said made sense, but it still made her heart hurt.

"We're going to slow down and be accessible. Okay?"

She nodded, reluctantly, and watched as he exited the vehicle. Haven seemed to talk to the front clerk for a long time, but he returned with a handful of keys, directing Copper to drive them around to the back of the building. They were on the ground floor, three rooms grouped together. "You're in the middle," he told her, handing her a key. "Copper and I will be there," he pointed to the right. "And Jibari and Dex will be there."

Donna nodded, knowing they were deliberately keeping her in the middle for safety reasons. Copper had backed the truck in, so they grabbed their go bags out of the back and headed to their respective rooms. Donna knew she would never be able to sleep, but it was nice to get into a space where she didn't have to always guard her expressions and feelings. She sank down onto the side of the sagging mattress, feeling desperately alone.

HAVEN COULD FEEL the misery from the next room, and he knew he needed to go check on Donna. It was funny because everyone was so scared of her, but right now she was just an angry, scared mother missing her daughter.

Krammer hadn't found them any new information, but he was working on it. Aiden had called in a few favors from places Haven probably didn't want to know about, but he hadn't heard anything either. They were in the dark, waiting for some kind of communication from McCullough.

Copper had stretched out on one of the beds, his booted feet crossed at the ankles and his arms folded behind his head. It would probably be smart for Haven to rest, too, but he was too wound. They'd headed south out of Alexandria, and they were now in the horse farms and hills of Virginia. If a person didn't want to be found, he could very easily disappear.

Haven sank down onto the side of the bed, for the first time feeling fatigue. They'd been running all day, and though he hadn't been the one driving, he had been scanning, constantly. Searching for power. His head felt like a lead balloon.

And if he felt this way, he expected Donna felt worse.

With that thought in mind, he called the front desk, looking for food. The guy said there was a homestyle restaurant just down the road and they would deliver. Haven called them and ordered a load of stuff, paying with the company card, then he crashed on the bed. He would just rest his eyes for a few minutes.

When there was a knock at the door, he answered it, taking the bags of food and tipping the delivery girl. Then he called the team into his room and unpacked the bags. He found the meal he ordered for himself and Donna, and he headed next door. She answered as soon as he knocked, and he held the styrofoam clamshells out to her. "I have a chicken tender salad or a meatloaf meal."

Her nose wrinkled, and he grinned slightly. That was a cute look on her.

"Salad, definitely," she said, waving him inside.

Donna led him onto the small, nondescript room, the late afternoon sun filtering through the old curtains. They ate in silence for a few minutes, the normalcy of the moment contrasting against their surreal day.

Haven studied her between bites, noting the shadows smudging her eyes and the fine lines of tension around her mouth. But her hand remained steady as she speared greens and chicken, drawing strength from the simple act of eating after so long without.

"How are you holding up?" he finally asked.

She paused, gazing out at the pines that edged the property. "I don't know. Each hour we lose the trail, my fears grow worse. But dwelling on them won't bring her back." Her eyes met his, bleak yet determined. "We have to stay focused. There is still hope as long as we keep hunting."

He reached across the table to squeeze her hand. "We will find her, Donna. I made you a promise to bring your daughter home, and I don't intend to break it."

A ghost of a smile touched her lips at the reminder, her fingers tightening on his. "I remember. And I'm holding you to your word." Her gaze dropped back to her salad. "Without that...I don't think I could keep going. This would break me." The admission was whispered, as if afraid to give the fear power by speaking it aloud.

Haven shifted his chair around to sit beside her, keeping her hand in his. "Then lean on me when you need to. I'm here to shoulder the weight so you can stay strong." His thumb rubbed over her knuckles, a small comfort. "You don't have to carry this alone anymore. We're partners, okay?"

She huffed a soft laugh. "Partners. Who would have imagined?"

But her body slowly relaxed into his side. "I just..."

She blinked, and there were tears in her eyes. Haven was alarmed, because she usually kept it together better than this. "What's wrong? What aren't you telling me?"

She shook her head and tried to pull her hand away, but he kept hold of her fingers.

"I don't dare speak the words," she whispered, "for fear of manifesting them."

*We have a loophole,* he said, speaking to her mentally.

That startled a laugh out of her, but just for a moment. Then her face collapsed into anguish. *I just... I wasn't treated well, there. And I'm terrified he will mistreat her.*

Anger spiked in him, and he thought he understood what she was saying. Did he dance around it and assume he knew? No, Donna was more direct than that. And there could be no misunderstandings. Haven tightened his hand on hers. *Donna, were you raped?*

Her emotions were clamped down, but there was a spike of rage from her. The entire room rattled, as if hit by a sonic boom. It was enough to push him back in the chair, but he continued to hold her hand. Haven didn't think she even realized what she'd done. His team began to move, but he sent them a mental all-clear, calling them off.

*Yes, I was. But they made sure to do it when the senator had dosed me with the drug and I was unaware. I would wake up and know, just know, that they'd done something. And the looks on their faces later.* She shook her head, disgust curling her lip. *But I took it. They knew I couldn't do anything against them. I wasn't as worried about the abuse as I was about Lilly.*

She glanced down at their hands, clamped together. Her fingers were white with tension, but he didn't think she even noticed.

*Roger would come down from the estate and tell me what a beautiful girl I had, and make me think he was grooming her for more. Like mother, like daughter, he would say.*

Haven fought with his own anger then. The lights flickered and one of his manifestations popped to life. This was an armored devil he had created in his imagination when they were doing a training exercise with Wulfe and Aiden. He called it Zed, because it was so wild. The menace that rolled off of it was something, though.

Donna jerked in alarm, then barked out a laugh. She glanced at him, appreciation in her eyes. *Thank you, Haven. I know you would protect me at all costs. Does he have a name?*

*Zed. He needed something a little unique.*

*Indeed.* Donna looked the creation over. *I have to say, if I met this in an alley I think I would pass out.*

Haven snorted, appreciating the admission. Yes, Zed was an interesting creature. *Aiden told me to create something completely foreign, and be able to keep him together for several minutes.*

Zed was not human. He was some hulking creature with arms almost to the ground, and claws of iron. There was a massive rifle slung over his back, but in his mind, Haven didn't feel like Zed needed it. Not when he had those claws. Zed's head was low on his shoulders, and a little stooped, but his eyes looked as hard as his claws. They were beady, with no whites, and very rarely blinked.

"How did you come up with him," she whispered.

Haven sighed, glad that she'd been distracted from her worry, but not happy about the topic. "There was a guard at the camp that liked to harass me. Big, strong guy that liked to hurt people. When it was my turn in the rotation, he always came to retrieve me. One night in my fever dreams he appeared to me like this. Hulking, menacing. That was when I started manifesting. I remember hearing men scream, and I looked up and the guard was there, and he'd pissed his pants. The form only stayed a few seconds, but it was enough to scare them all. I started laughing at him, and that was when I found myself on the very edge of the camp, barely cared for."

"Damn," she breathed.

Haven let the manifestation disappear in a wisp of imaginary smoke. It was telling that he'd brought him out for her.

Donna sighed, leaning back in her chair. "Thank you for the distraction. I know I get caught up in a loop in my head. But if McCullough so much as touches a hair on that girl's head, he's going to die a horrible death."

Haven snorted. "I remember what you did to some of the others."

When they'd broken Lilly and Donna out of the senator's care, there had been some casualties at the senator's penthouse, where he'd kept Donna. Three random soldiers were found dead with unexplainable wounds. Two had broken necks, and one had been gutted. None of their team had done it, and no one had taken responsibility. They put it down as a couple of enhanced guards that had escaped. Or maybe fought their way out of the apartment. They knew that the senator had several enhanced men working for him. Donna knew of a dozen, at least. Only about seven had been accounted for, and they were either dead or incarcerated after Donna had made them null.

So, they had five enhanced soldiers in the wind that they

knew of, not including McCullough. One of the men may have been the dead body in the alley they hadn't identified yet, but he kind of doubted it. If they were enhanced, McCullough knew how valuable they were. He wouldn't kill them on a whim. And Dex had said he smelled wrong, like it hadn't taken.

Actually, he was assuming a lot about McCullough right now. And he was assuming they knew how many enhanced men were out there. Even though the senator was incarcerated, Haven seriously doubted that he was done in the espionage business. There could be hundreds of enhanced men out there, and they just didn't know.

The thought sent a chill through him. Because without Donna's help to shape their minds, there could be homicidal menaces walking the streets.

"What is that scowl for?" Donna murmured.

Haven blinked and looked up at her. He shook his head, sighing. "Just wondering what kind of monsters we have to look forward to, besides McCullough."

Donna sighed, looking resigned. "Two of the men missing are as bad as if not worse than McCullough. McCullough has a goal. I feel like he wants me back for a payday, and then I think he wants to get out of Dodge and go hide somewhere. He never had patience with the senator or his employees. But there were two... they were just nasty. And not right in the head. Andre Solana and Michael Wilson. If I could have wiped them and gotten away with it I would have. They never should have been given the drug in the first place."

"I have a feeling we're going to find more men like that, since one vial is still missing. It could be anywhere, and if it's in the wrong hands, they're already breaking down the formula."

"Yes," she sighed. "I told the government that, but I don't think they understand the scope of what could happen."

They looked at each other, knowing how bad it really could be.

"It's not something we can deal with right now," Haven said eventually. "I know you don't want to hear this, but you need to try to sleep."

Donna looked back out the window. "I don't think I can."

"Can you lay down and fake it for me?"

That startled a laugh out of her, and turned her cheeks pink. Haven blinked and winced. "That's not what I meant."

Donna faced him. "I know, Haven. That's what makes you so precious. You're not tap-dancing around my feelings or what happened to me."

"No, I'm just blundering around like an idiot. I'm sorry."

Donna leaned forward and pressed a kiss to his forehead, before she stood from the chair. "Maybe I'll try."

Haven watched her disappear into the bathroom, and he wondered if it was time for him to leave. He gathered up their trash and bagged it, then set it by the door. He could take it when he left. Moving to the window, he looked out into the night. Though he couldn't see him, Jibari was somewhere to the east, circling the building. Haven knew he probably wouldn't be able to sleep in a place like this, so he would keep watch over them all.

It felt like Copper and Dex were both out. They knew to take sleep when they were able.

Donna came out of the bathroom, and Haven blinked, shocked. As quick as he could, he slammed a mental shield down on his thoughts, but Donna smiled anyway, lifting her chin to look at him. She was freshly showered, her face pink from the heat of the water. What had grabbed him, though, was her hair. It was long, almost down to her waist, and such a beautiful black. It was wet, which made it darker of course, and there was some curl to it. The look was such a departure from her normal bun that it staggered him a little. And it caused a completely inappropriate reaction in him. The vision of her over top of him had popped into his head almost immediately, her hair curtaining them both.

"I'm sorry," he said immediately, knowing he'd been completely open and that she'd probably seen what he wanted.

Donna shook her head. "I'm not, Haven. That was beautiful. And, truth be told, I'm glad you know about... everything now. don't feel like I have a lot of trauma associated with the rapes themselves, it was the loss of control," she fisted her hands, and her voice quavered at the end. "I remember the senator pushing the button on that damn watch, and the smirks on the men's faces as they let me fall. Once I was sedated, I don't remember anything. But when the senator let me out, and I opened up my mind, the thoughts were there in their minds to be read. I was so furious at the way they viewed me, like I was a piece of furniture to be used and discarded."

Haven felt the room flex around him, and he knew it was her anger. "Did you kill those other three men?"

"I did," she said immediately, her gaze clear as she met his look. "They used me every chance they got, and they bragged about it, talked about it. I made sure they died horrible deaths."

Haven let her feel his satisfaction at her ability to take care of herself, and she grinned at him. It was the first time he'd ever seen that expression on her face, and he loved it.

"I thought you would be disappointed in me," she murmured, her mouth quivering as she sat on the edge of the bed. Her dark eyes were huge in her pale face.

"Why on Earth would I be disappointed with you?" he growled. "You fought back, exactly the way you're supposed to. We're Army, woman, and you did your service proud."

She stared at him for a long moment, before she burst

into tears. Haven was so shocked that he didn't know what to do. "I'm sorry," he murmured, crossing to the bed. He sank down onto the edge, then wrapped an arm around her shoulders. He tried to keep the movement as sexless as possible, just one friend comforting another. But she turned into his embrace, and he was helpless but to reciprocate.

Haven held Donna as she cried, and he stroked her wet hair. "You're okay," he murmured, over and over again. "I won't let them hurt you again," he promised.

She wrapped both arms around him, sagging into him, and Haven did his best to console her. He was a little shocked that she trusted him enough to be this vulnerable. Donna was such a control freak.

Then she did something completely unexpected. Drawing back, she looked up into his eyes, leaned forward and kissed the shit out of him.

Haven was shocked for a minute and he didn't know what to do. He was already holding her, but his hands shifted, cupping her face. The taste of her tears was haunting, but it didn't deter him at all. He'd been hungry for her for so long. Then she really shocked him as she moved to straddle his hips.

Haven gasped at the feel of her warm body connecting with his so intimately. Immediately, he hardened against that heat. He'd been fine comforting her when she'd been upset, but she'd just turned the boat in a completely different direction and hit the throttle. He pulled back from the kiss to look into her face. "Donna," he whispered, but he was unable to say more.

His mind was wide open to her, and for the first time, hers was open to him as well. This close, there was no shielding what the other was feeling, and he got a bit of insight. She was desperate to feel normal. Desperate to feel more than pain and fear. Everyone treated her like she was made of spun glass, or a pariah, and she tried not to respond, but it was so painful. Sometimes she wanted to just lash out and make them feel the pain she did.

Cupping her cheeks, he looked into her eyes. "I understand. But I've never looked at you that way."

Her face crumpled into tears again, and he wrapped his arms around her, just holding her as she cried. He understood why she'd kissed him like that, and straddled his lap. She'd wanted his honest, shocked reaction so that she could read him. And he'd given it to her.

Even though he hadn't felt the same reaction from her.

DONNA HAD SO many emotions rolling through her. She couldn't believe she'd acted the way she had, but it was done now. And he'd behaved like a gentleman, in spite of the way she'd ambushed him. He deserved so much more than her. She slid from his lap, walking to the bathroom door.

"Haven, I'm sorry."

He looked at her, his eyes clear, and smiled at her slightly. "There's nothing to be sorry about."

She shook her head, dark hair swinging. "I disagree. I'm not... rational right now. You deserve better than that."

Haven stood, crossed the room to her and cupped her shoulders. "I think we both deserve better."

She blinked and nodded. Yes, he was very right about that. She allowed him to wrap her in his arms, and she rested her head against his chest. The beat of his heart was strong, and she loved listening to it.

"When we get out of this mess," he continued, voice rumbling through his chest, "we're going on a date."

Donna blinked and looked up at him, the concept was so

foreign. Then it intrigued her, just a little. "And where would we go, you and I, on this date?"

"It doesn't matter. Maybe we'll escape to the kitchen and have Nicole cook us an elaborate pizza."

Donna barked out a laugh, resting her head on his chest again. "I'm afraid I might be pizza-ed out."

"Then I'll get an MRE from the stock room. That will really knock your socks off."

Donna snickered, running her hands over his chest, then around his waist. It felt very nice to be held. And the thought of going on a date with him seemed... intriguing. "Okay," she said softly. "Once we get out of this, I'll go on a date with you."

Haven leaned back enough to catch her eye, grinning down at her. "I'm going to hold you to it."

She nodded, her heart aching.

"Let's go lay down. Completely platonic, I promise. We both need sleep, and I'd like to hold you like this for a while if you'll let me."

The thought should have terrified her, but this was Haven. She knew the man's mind just as well as her own, and he'd never had inappropriate thoughts about her. He'd been aroused by her. She'd felt that many times from him. But he knew her situation and he knew she wasn't in a place to accept him in any way but platonic. Hesitantly, she nodded.

They settled into bed, she going to the right side and he to the left, naturally, like they'd done it for years. Then they each turned onto their left sides, spooning. Haven kept space between their hips, but he rested his arm along the length of her thigh. Donna sagged into the mattress, her body immediately relaxing. She loved the feel of his heat along her back, and she had no fear of him. She had worried that her psyche would throw up red flags when she lay down with him, but her heart rate was steady and she didn't feel any anxiety toward him.

One of his hands raised, and he began stroking her damp hair back from her head. Donna closed her eyes and accepted the touch, feeling her bones melt. This man was doing everything he could to relax her, and she appreciated the hell out of him for it.

She let herself float, her breathing deepening, and she let go. He would protect her from everything.

## 11

L illy was tired of being a passenger. And she was tired of looking at the back of this guy's head. But she was afraid for whatever would come when he stopped.

Roger McCullough had been a dick when he worked for the senator. And he was still a dick now. Time and distance hadn't changed him. He was looking kind of ragged, though. His dark hair used to be super short. Now it was longer, like he hadn't seen a barber in a long time. And he had bags under his eyes.

Good. He deserved to look like this. He'd stolen her away from the only home she had.

She looked out the window. Nothing looked familiar, of course. They'd been traveling on back roads for hours, mostly through hilly farm country, and she knew for a fact he'd done at least a few circles. Some of the roads she recognized from the hour before. Or even minutes before. The light was fading. The sun was sinking below the trees to her right, she she knew they were heading south. She thought they might still be in Virginia. Or maybe North Carolina. It was close, right? The road signs had changed a while ago, and she tried not to appear too interested. Right now, he thought she was just an airhead teenager. She wanted him to keep thinking that.

"I have to poop. And I'm hungry."

He spared her a glance through the rearview mirror, and she lifted her brows at him. "It's been hours!" she moaned dramatically.

"It actually hasn't been. You went two hours ago."

"Yeah," she said with sass. "Hours, like I said."

He scowled at her, but within half an hour he was pulling into an old service station. The thing looked like it was out of the sixties, or something. It was old and covered in rusty tin. She wasn't even sure it was open. Then she saw an old man sitting outside in an even older looking chair. Before they got out of the car, McCullough leaned around over the seat. He cut the cable tie from her wrists with a knife and stared her in the eye. "Listen to me, little girl. You're going to behave and not raise suspicion. Do you understand?"

She gave him a mocking salute. "Yes, sir!"

She waited for him to let her out of the older car he'd stolen. It was almost as beat up and disgusting as the service station. "If they don't have a decent bathroom here, you're gonna have to take me somewhere else," she hissed up at him.

Roger McCullough gave her a dark look. "Go take your shit. And don't make me regret letting you out."

Lilly walked across to the old man. He seemed half asleep. Or maybe half dead. "Do you have a restroom, sir?"

"In the back," he rumbled.

Lilly went through the store. It looked like it had fallen out of the sky and just landed here. The floors were wavy with age, and old wood. She paused to look at the shelves. Everything was covered in dust. Ew...

She found the bathroom in the back of the store, and it actually had working plumbing. She was scared it was going to be an outhouse. As soon as she got inside and locked the door, she pulled her phone from her sock. Her hands shook as she held the phone up. They were in the middle of nowhere and there was a very good chance she had no service.

The screen lit up and all five bars lit, then disappeared. She held her arm up to the little square window in the corner, and one bar popped up. Okay, she would type her text, then hold it to the window when she sent it.

*Mom, I'm ok. In NC I think. Pee break. In a dk blue olds cutlass. Stank ass car. AP3959. I love you. He hasn't hurt me and he hasn't said where we're going. Will keep phone as long as possible.*

She hit send, and nothing happened immediately. She went to the window and held the phone up, praying that she had bars. A message popped up on the screen that the message would be sent when she had service. Well, okay. That would have to do. She made sure it was silent, then tucked it securely back into her sock. Then she used the bathroom, making sure to take a little extra time just because. When she came out of the bathroom, Roger was standing there, staring at her.

"What?" she snapped.

Brushing by her, he stepped into the bathroom and looked around. She thought he might have been looking for a note she'd left or something. She watched him go through the bathroom, and shook her head. Let him look. There was nothing there.

Turning, she wandered through the aisles, looking for something to eat. There was nothing in here she wanted to put in her mouth. Finally, she found a can of cashews that were sealed and not out of date. She put them on the counter for McCullough to buy, then added a bottle of pop. He gave her a look as he paid for the items, then grabbed her arm and headed out to the car.

"I can walk, asshole," she hissed. "And if you don't want to draw attention, you need to let me."

He let her go, but he gave her a menacing look. "Get in."

She went to the car and popped the driver's side seat lever so she could climb in the back. She led with her foot with the phone in the sock, just in case. He slammed the seat back and climbed in, started the car and pulled away from the pumps. They started down the busy road, but he pulled over once he was out of view from the station. "Give me your wrists."

He produced a zip tie from somewhere, and Lilly drew back against the seat. "Seriously?" she growled. "What am I going to do? I know how to be a prisoner. I was a prisoner for three years, remember?"

He gave her a long look. "You'd better not give me any problems."

"I won't. Give me my snacks."

He tossed them over the seat to her, then shifted back into gear and accelerated. Lilly tried not to cheer as she ripped the can open and started eating her dinner. Then she curled up on her side on the bench seat and went to sleep, the sound of pavement lulling her to sleep.

DONNA BLINKED awake when she heard the buzz of her phone. It was after one am, and she'd actually been asleep. Ah, that was why. Haven was curled up on his side beside her, snoring lightly. She smiled as she looked at him. He was a good hearted guy, and she felt guilty for treating him the way she had last night. She was so leery of trusting, though. The men in her life had never treated her well, and it was a struggle to think about letting another one in. Haven was not pushing her, at all, but she knew there was some expectation there.

And some part of her wanted what she thought he might be offering. If she could just trust him enough... In a way, she already did. Hell, she was in bed with the man. After what she'd gone through that was a huge step.

Reaching for the phone, she swiped the screen, blinking. Then she gasped and peered closer.

"Haven!"

He was beside her in an instant, leaning over her shoulder to see the message. At almost the same time his phone went off. "That's probably Krammer."

The tech was relating the same message.

*Mom, I'm ok. In NC I think. Pee break. In a dk blue olds cutlass. Stank ass car. AP3959. I love you. He hasn't hurt me and he hasn't said where we're going. Will keep phone as long as possible.*

Donna's fingers flew as she sent a succinct response. *Noted. Stay safe however you can, baby! I love you. Message when you can.*

Haven squeezed her shoulder as he read her message, and Donna clutched at his hand. The relief she felt was so strong, it almost overwhelmed her. Tears burned in her eyes. "Can we go after her? She has to be so scared."

Haven shifted on the bed beside her. "We're probably going to send a team down to that coordinate, but we're going to wait. I know it's hard, but he's not done driving, yet. We're going to give him time to settle. He must have a destination in mind."

Donna winced, but she knew he was right. If they ran down there now, Lilly wouldn't be there. It had just been a break. They needed to wait for him to stop. She turned, unable to hold the tears in any longer. Haven immediately wrapped her in his arms, and the pain eased just a little.

"It will be okay, Donna. She's an incredibly smart kid, and we have teams on standby." His phone buzzed, and he looked down. "Wulfe has arranged for a chopper to be on standby. It will meet us as soon as we give the word, and it will get us wherever we need to go."

She rocked her head against his chest, glad that someone was keeping it together better than she was. "I'm sorry," she said, drawing away. She swiped at her tears angrily, hating the loss of control.

Haven stilled her hands. "Stop, Donna. It's okay to feel this emotion, and it doesn't make you weaker. At least, not in my eyes."

Donna went still, looking down at their joined hands. They had seen a lot of damage. Haven was a worker. There were scars crisscrossing his fingers and the backs of his hands. One nail was black from some injury and they were all a little ragged. But his grip was strong, and she knew he would never let her go. And when she lifted her gaze to his, that same strength was there in the solidness of his gaze. There was no guile there, just support, and she didn't understand why he'd thrown his lot in with hers. For them. "Haven, you don't owe me anything anymore. You never did. When I helped you, I did it for my own reasons, to get out of that penthouse."

He gave her a crooked smile. "I know that. And as much as I appreciated what you did for me, it's definitely not why I'm helping you now."

She blinked, frowning. "I know why you're helping me. You have to. You're part of the Dogs of War's team, and they want to keep me happy."

Haven frowned, a crooked smile on his face. "That's definitely not why I'm doing it."

"I don't understand, then. Why?"

"Because I'm nuts about you, woman, and I'm waiting for you to realize what's standing right in front of you."

That sat her back. Donna drew her hands out of Haven's, and one went up to cover her mouth. Then she shook her head, slipping off the bed. "I can't do this right now."

Haven gave her a chagrined smile. "I know. I shouldn't have told you that way. My timing is perfect, once again. Just forget I said anything." Slipping from the bed, he headed to the door. "I'm going to go check in with the team, let them know what's going on."

And he left.

Donna blinked, wondering at the craziness of her life. It should have settled down considering she was no longer the hostage of a madman.

She sank down onto the bed again. The last five minutes had been... well, just manic. That was the only word that came to mind. She'd loved laying with Haven, but now she wanted to scream and cry.

Lilly was safe as of this moment, though. That was the most important thing. Now it was just a game of waiting. Wait for McCullough to go to ground, wait for Lilly to contact them again. Or wait for Krammer to unearth some obscure detail that only he would see.

Then once something happened, they needed to wait for the helicopter. There was no way Haven was leaving her behind when they went after her daughter.

Haven. The man made her head spin, and not necessarily in a good way. He'd been there for them in a lot of small ways, making sure they settled in right, and making sure Lilly had everything she needed. And he'd been there for her in big ways, urging her to come out of her shell in more ways than one. He'd made her realize that she couldn't stay cloistered. It wasn't healthy for her or Lilly. She appreciated him, more than she'd ever told him.

And now that he had left her room, she wanted him to come back.

## 12

I t was a long night. There were no more messages from Lilly. Krammer was watching traffic cams, but it would be like searching for a needle in a haystack. A blue Cutlass. Old enough that there was no GPS in the car to track.

Haven wished she'd said something about Roger. Had he changed his hair color or grown out a beard? Something to narrow down the search parameters.

Roger McCullough was a smart ass mother fucker. He'd made it through Damon Wilkes and Senator Hall, and now he was enterprising for himself. The Dogs of War knew that Nicholas Pike, an intern, was handling the former senator's affairs, but Haven couldn't imagine McCullough taking orders from Pike. Maybe McCullough was in contact with one of Hall's other associates. There was an entire vial of Marathon missing. Someone had it, and was probably using it, but they didn't know who.

Haven knew they wanted Belladonna back, which was why Lilly had been taken. Belladonna would streamline their enterprise and help shape the test subjects. It wasn't what she wanted to do, though. She'd settled into her nursing job at the

Elton building and seemed to enjoy it. She was working on the second floor, where the more critically ill patients were. Haven knew that Dr. Cole valued Donna's professional experience, and that every single one of her patients had responded to her.

"You need sleep," Copper grumbled.

Haven rolled his head to look at him. The night was dark, but he could see Copper's strong profile in the light from a street lamp. "I know," Haven murmured.

He was tired, but so much had happened in the past few hours. He was wound up like a top. It didn't feel right, being this far away from Donna. She'd needed space, though, after he'd inelegantly dropped his bombshell.

Why the hell had he told her that he wanted to be with her? She wasn't ready to hear anything like it, and they certainly weren't in a situation to act on anything. Her daughter was missing. That was what they needed to concentrate on.

Haven rolled to his side, senses reaching into the night. Jibari had completed his rounds and now Dex was out there, on the lookout for anything out of the ordinary. They were in the middle of nowhere, and he doubted they had a tail. It was good to be safe, though.

Haven drifted off to sleep, but it seemed like mere minutes later when Copper roused. It was his turn for guard duty. Haven watched with half an eye open as his buddy let himself out of the room. Copper was one of the best former soldiers he knew, and nothing would get by him.

Haven slept for a couple more hours, then roused when Copper called to him, mentally. *We've got a car cruising through that feels a little weird.*

Haven levered up out of bed, his senses ranging out. Yes, there it was. It wasn't a feeling like his own men, but he definitely felt a mind that was enhanced. *Can you see the driver?*

*No. The windows are blacked out. I'm on the south side of the building and he's gone through twice. Maybe I'm feeling something that isn't there.*

*No, I feel it too. And if I feel them, they can probably feel us.*

As if they heard Haven's mental message, the sedan accelerated out of the lot and turned right, speeding away from the hotel.

*Pack up,* Haven called to his men. *We're moving. I'll tell Donna.*

He left his room and headed next door. She answered the door as soon as he called out. "I felt them as soon as they rolled into the lot. Where did they go?"

Haven shook his head. "Not sure. They just tore out of the lot. I need you to get your bag together. We're moving."

She nodded and turned back to the room. He went back to his own room and shoved his toothbrush in his go bag. It was still mostly packed, because he hadn't showered yet. He'd have to shower at the next stop.

Within five minutes they were all loaded in the SUV and heading down the road. They weren't necessarily trying to chase down the mercenaries in the suspicious car, but if it was pulled over, they might have to have a conversation with the gentlemen inside. They needed to figure out who they were.

"Did they feel familiar?" Haven asked Donna, turning slightly in his seat.

She made a bit of a face. "Kind of, but not exactly. I don't know how to explain it. Like, I've felt the flavor of the enhancement, but not them specifically."

Haven nodded, understanding the feeling. "It's alright. We'll keep moving and stay alert. We'll figure out who they are soon enough."

They drove for an hour, stopping once for a quick food break and gas. Haven made sure to choose a gas station that was relatively busy, with plenty of people and cameras around.

As they got back on the road, Haven's mind drifted to the missing vial of Marathon and Roger McCullough. Roger didn't have the vial. Of that, he was certain. Roger wouldn't have gone through with the kidnapping if he had the vial. The drug was worth so much more than Lilly. And he had the connections to implement the sale.

"Haven," Donna's voice broke into his thoughts. "I've been thinking."

He turned to her, noting the serious expression on her face. "What is it?"

Donna glanced at the men beside her. He felt the brush of her mind on his own, so he dropped his defenses for her. *What is it, Donna?*

She blinked, looking down at her hands, then back up. *I just wanted to let you know how much I appreciate you letting me come with you to get Lilly. I know I'm still building bridges with the team, and I appreciate the chance to do that.*

*Of course. I want you to work well with my team. Any of these men would give their lives for you. And for Lilly.*

Her lips pursed, and she looked down at her hands again, fiddling with her fingernail. *I know. I can feel that from them, and it's very humbling.*

*I have a feeling if the shit hits the fan, you won't be standing idly by.*

A grin tugged one corner of her mouth and she looked up, meeting his gaze. *You are correct.*

Haven appreciated her bloodthirsty expression. With a wink, he turned back around in his seat.

Their conversation seemed to be timely. A few minutes later they cruised into a small town. They were passing under a railroad underpass when Donna said, "Haven! I think I feel..."

That was all she got out before their vehicle was slammed violently in the side.

The big SUV went spinning. Traffic had been light, so they didn't hit anyone else, but they slammed into the buttress of the underpass. The SUV came to an abrupt, rocking stop, and they all swayed to the right. Haven's head bounced off the window, ringing his bell, but he righted himself quickly. Blinking, he turned around in his seat, waiting to feel pain.

Jibari and Copper had taken the brunt of the impact. Jibari was out cold, the passenger area where he'd been sitting crumpled in toward Donna. Copper was moaning, slumped forward against the steering wheel. Haven glanced at Donna. "Are you okay?"

She nodded, holding Jibari across her lap. "I'm fine. They braced me. Go!"

Haven glanced at Dex. "You all right?"

Dex nodded, gun in hand. There was blood on his temple, but he seemed clear-eyed as he glanced between the front and the back windows. "We're sitting ducks. We need to get out of here."

"You go out the back and I'll go out the front."

Haven pivoted in his seat, unlocked his seatbelt and swung his feet up. He kicked at the cracked windshield. This wasn't an armored vehicle, so it popped out fairly easily with a few focused hits.

"There are two of them," Donna called out. "Both enhanced."

Gunfire began to pelt the vehicle. Fuck. He wasn't surprised, but he didn't like it. Haven scrambled out through the opening he'd created, and shimmied down the hood, taking cover in front of the bumper. Then he pulled his own weapon. When there was a break in the gunfire, he peered out, looking for the driver. Hopefully, when the mercs had hit them, they had injured themselves as well. He couldn't count on that, but he could hope for it.

And now that Donna had confirmed the men were enhanced, he could feel them. The driver was panicking. Their sedan wasn't as well-built as the SUV, and his foot was trapped. Gunfire ripped from the merc's side window, though, and Haven knew the guy wasn't thinking straight. He was panicking, knowing he was about to die. Haven couldn't tell what the man's specialty was. It just felt like he'd been given a heavy dose of adrenalin, or something. There was no focus. Just vague power. Which didn't really mean anything to Haven in a fight.

Haven built three heavily armed soldiers off to the right to draw gunfire away from himself. The addled driver had to be wondering where they'd come from and why he wasn't hitting anyone. Then the gun clicked empty. Haven peered through the smoke and sighted down his own barrel. "You're done."

The man put his hands up in submission, his face furious. That was easy enough.

Dex had taken care of his own man, who was on the ground, hands zip-tied behind his back. Dex covered Haven as he pulled the driver from the smashed sedan. He'd have ripped the guy's leg off if it hadn't come free, but it let loose when he twisted. The man cried out, but Haven didn't care.

"What the fuck were you thinking?" Haven demanded.

"Fuck you," the man growled, snarling up at him.

Haven zipped his hands together behind his back, then sat him up. Sirens were wailing, and he knew they were running out of time to get information.

"Who do you work for," he asked, but he had a feeling he already knew.

"Fuck you," the man said again, resting his head down onto the wet concrete.

Grinning, Haven planted a fist in the man's ugly face. "You're going to wish you'd talked to me."

Blood gushed from the man's nose, but he didn't say anything. Haven was about to turn away when the man tried to attack his mind. When he turned to look, the guy was snarling, and very obviously seemed to be trying to hurt him, but the attempt was weak. "Seriously?"

Haven turned and walked away, not even responding to the attack. He had injured men to check on.

Jibari had taken the brunt of the impact, but there was a side-curtain airbag that cushioned some of it. Donna had found the medical kit they kept in back, and was doing her best to stop the bleeding from his temple. When Haven ducked his head inside, she shook her head. "I've got him. You check on Copper."

Copper was already beginning to rouse. The man had a very hard head, which Haven could attest to. There were small scratches all over his broad face, though. Probably from the glass from his window being smashed into his face by the airbag. Even as he watched, Copper opened his pale eyes and glanced around. Haven grinned at him. "Hey, big man."

Copper groaned, lifting a hand to his face. *Don't touch. You have glass in your skin.*

Copper grimaced and rocked his head back against the headrest. "I did not expect that."

"None of us did," Haven said, speaking a little louder over the sirens. "Are your legs okay?"

Copper made a movement inside the space. "Yeah, seems fine. Jib okay?"

"Banged up but Donna is working on him."

A firetruck and an ambulance pulled up. Men started tumbling out and going for supplies.

Haven looked at Donna. "I know you're busy, but any chance you can scan the merc's minds real quick?"

Donna blinked at him, then looked at the men on the ground outside. She stared at them, hard, a frown wrinkling her brow. She tilted her head, focusing, them looked at him. "They aren't the ones from the warehouse or the penthouse. I don't recognize these men."

"Fuck," Haven breathed. Now they had even more questions than answers.

JIBARI WAS PLACED ONTO A BACKBOARD, a brace around his neck. It was bitterly cold, and Haven hoped they got him into the rig quickly. His hot-blooded friend didn't like the cold.

Haven contacted Wulfe, and Dr. Cole would be on the chopper as soon as they could get her there. The little podunk town could stabilize Jibari, but she didn't want them doing any further care that she didn't personally oversee.

The cops arrived, and Haven had to pull out his handy, dandy get out of jail free card, aka CIA credentials. Because he was a part of Joint Task Force Omega, it pinged on his record when he was ran. When any of them were ran. And it gave him police authority. When the local cops made noises about releasing the two mercs from their restraints, Haven had to remind them that the men were in his custody. Of course they had to call in a supervisor, and then she had to call her supervisor, because it wasn't a situation they'd ever dealt with.

Kevin Rose eventually called him, and Haven could tell he was frustrated. "What the hell did you get into, Haven?"

Haven snorted. "Well, you know about the kidnapping. Someone did a drive-by of our hotel this morning, so we bugged out. Little did we know these fuckers were waiting to T-bone us in this backwater town. We're in Weldon, North

Carolina. Jibari is on his way to the hospital, Dr. Cole is on her way down, and Copper is giving the ambulance team fits. We have two tangos in custody. The medics have checked them out and they have scrapes and abrasions, but nothing more than that. Donna scanned them, and she doesn't recognize them. As soon as we can settle, we're going to let her deep dive into their minds and figure out who the fuck they are."

Rose sighed, sounding put-upon. "Okay, keep me posted. You and Donna are okay?"

"Yes, I think so. Jibari took the brunt of the hit. Copper's face is a mess, but he's okay. Two female paramedics are working on him now. Dex went to go grab a car."

"No word from McCullough?"

"No. You know about the text from Lilly, right?"

"Yes."

Of course he did. He was the CIA.

"Keep me posted on what Donna figures out."

"Will do."

Haven answered a call from Wulfe next, and went over the same details. "Sorry, boss man. Truck is totaled."

"Fuck the truck! I'm not worried about that," Wulfe said. "I'm just glad you guys are okay. I'm sending a team of Deltas with Elizabeth when she comes down."

"I think that would be prudent."

Haven thought about the men left in the Elton building. Two days ago they'd had plenty of men, but now that shit was going down, they were severely exposed. That was probably why Wulfe was staying there. Aiden and Angela's baby had been targeted mere days ago, and if they redirected more men, there was a possibility Hall's compatriots could just waltz in and steal her. Or wipe out the injured men. Or destroy the building. Haven knew that Wulfe and Aiden would do everything in their power to protect their home.

There were men in training, but they were not ready for a full-out assault.

"It might not be a bad idea to pad the security at the building, somehow. Even if you have to call Holtman for some back-up."

"I'll see what I can do on short notice," Wulfe said, sighing heavily. "Keep me updated."

And he hung up.

Finally, Haven was able to go to Donna. She was standing at the edge of the curb, looking badass in her formfitting jacket, with the holster at her hip. She was watching the medics load Jibari into the back of the ambulance, her arms crossed over her stomach. There was blood on her hands, and she held them away from her body in a practiced move. Without giving her a chance to move away, Haven wrapped an arm around her shoulders for a hug and looked down at her. "He'll be okay."

"Yes, I know. He did have a brain bleed, but I got it stopped. Now he's just unconscious. As long as he doesn't swell too bad, he should be okay in a couple of days."

She leaned into his hold, sagging a little. Haven appreciated that tiny bit of control she'd just given up.

"Let's find a place to settle and get you cleaned up."

Dex had arrived with a different SUV, in dark blue. Haven dragged the merc driver around to the back. Dex was going to have to drive, and Haven would have to keep the mercs under control.

As soon as one of the men saw Donna, though, his entire demeanor changed. "I know you," he panted, his eyes going wide. "Don't kill me. I have information, I swear."

Donna reached out and rested a hand on the struggling man's head, knocking him out instantly. The second man looked at her impassively, and passed out just as easy with her touch. "Now we don't have to worry about watching them. They'll sleep until I wake them up."

Haven and Dex threw the two men into the back of the rented SUV. "There's a motel near the hospital," Dex said. "Secluded and near the highway."

Haven nodded, looking over at Copper. The medics had been working on his face for about twenty minutes, and they wanted to take him to the hospital, but Copper refused. Haven didn't blame the man. He wouldn't choose to go to an unfamiliar hospital either. But as soon as they were settled and a little rested, one of them needed to go to the hospital so that Jibari didn't wake up alone.

Once the medics were done with Copper, they loaded up into the rented vehicle and headed to the motel Dex had found. Then, with two adjoining rooms, they took a few minutes to relax. They carried the mercenaries in, dumping them on the floor of one of the rooms, then Copper crashed on one of the beds with a groan. Haven could feel the pain he was in, and wished he had a way to ease it for his friend.

Donna went into the adjoining room and grabbed her bag. "If you don't mind, I'm going to take a quick shower to get the blood and glass off me."

"Go ahead," he told her. "I'll take one after you."

She nodded once, then closed the adjoining door.

Haven didn't like the look in her eyes. She'd been withdrawn since the wreck. Yes, it could be from the wreck itself, that was always a scare. But he thought it was from the way the driver had reacted to her. He'd recognized her, and known what she could do.

DONNA KNEW she needed to get her head in the game, but she was rattled. It had been more than a year since anyone had looked at her like that, and she didn't miss the feeling. It made her feel terrible, knowing what she'd done for the senator and Dr. Shu. She'd had such hope when she'd first started, because the possibilities of the serum were immense. *If* it was used correctly.

She'd moved on, though, and she was living the life she wanted with her daughter. At some point they would think about starting a life of their own, away from the Dogs of War and the CIA. She was indebted to everything that they'd done for her, but change was coming. She felt like she'd changed by leaps and bounds from a year ago. Lilly had very obviously changed. Yeah, they were still isolated from the rest of the world in a way, but at this time, it was for the best.

At some point they would break away and create a home for themselves. At least, that was the plan. She was making a good wage right now, and banking most of it because she was staying at the Elton building. She had no expenses.

Maybe they could find an old farmhouse somewhere. Something that needed to be fixed up. She would love to have a garden. Donna looked down at her hands. They'd wreaked so much havoc over the years. It would be nice if they could create something beautiful, as well.

Shaking her head at her fanciful thoughts, she reached for the hair brush. Her hair was a mass of tangles, and it took her longer than normal to brush them out. Her phone was on the charger on the other room, and she checked it as soon as she walked in. Nothing. She fought her anxiety as she set the phone down. Lilly just hadn't gotten to a place where she could safely text. She would as soon as possible. Lilly had no love for McCullough either.

Frustration bubbled in her gut, building, and she fought not to fling power out to destroy something. Her control was frazzled.

There was a knock on the adjoining door. Of course he

would come to her now. The man was like a damned radar to her emotions.

"Come in," she said, crossing her arms beneath her breasts. She was standing at the window, and she turned as Haven walked into the room. Those dark eyes scanned her from head to toe, lingering on the damp hair hanging over her shoulder.

"Every time I see your hair, I'm surprised at how long it is. How do you keep it up in that bun?"

Donna snorted, fingering the strands. "Well, you just keep winding and winding, and twist it around itself before you tuck it and add an elastic band."

Haven took a couple of steps closer to her, head tilted to the side. His voice softened. "You know, you don't have to keep everything bottled up, Donna. I can see that something's bothering you. Talk to me."

Donna sighed, feeling a mix of frustration and vulnerability. She felt exposed, that he could read her so easily. "It's just... Lilly. She's been radio silent for hours. I know she can't always reach out, but my anxiety is getting the best of me."

Haven's expression turned serious. "I understand your worry, Donna. We're doing everything we can to find McCullough and keep you safe. But sometimes, we need to trust that the people we care about will do what they need to do. Your daughter is a kick ass little human. Remember, she put Copper on the training mat just a few weeks ago."

Donna looked down, her fingers nervously fidgeting with the hem of her shirt. "I know... it's just hard. Especially when I feel this connection with Lilly, and yet, I'm still afraid."

Haven closed the remaining distance between them, gently placing a hand on Donna's arm. "I get it. Fear is a natural response, especially when we care deeply about someone. But you're not alone in this. We'll find Lilly, and we'll face whatever comes our way together."

Donna met Haven's gaze, finding reassurance in his eyes. The man was giving her hope, but she wasn't sure she could trust it. "Thank you, Haven. I appreciate your support. I don't know what I would do without you."

Haven's voice was filled with sincerity. "We're a team. And together, we'll get her back."

As they stood there, sharing a moment of understanding, Donna felt a surge of determination. She knew she had to trust in their abilities and lean on Haven for support. They would bring Lilly home safely.

She looked up at him, scanning his face. He'd taken some damage in the crash. There were a couple of small scratches on his left cheekbone. She ran her fingers over them, but she could see they were already healing. "When I think of what McCullough has cost us, I get very angry."

Haven blinked down at her, smiling slightly. "I know. And you're going to have to use that anger in a bit. I'm going to get cleaned up, then we're going to get some answers from those men. You with me?"

Donna nodded, smiling slightly. Haven stepped forward and wrapped her in his arms, giving her a quick hug.

"I'll be back, and we'll go kick some ass."

She nodded and watched as he walked into the bathroom with his go-bag. Yes, maybe kicking some ass would make her feel better. Or maybe another Haven hug...

## 13

L illy looked up at the cabin, and scowled. This was going to suck. They were literally in the middle of nowhere, yet this seemed to be McCullough's destination. The cabin was decent sized, but the driveway was overgrown. There were wires attached to the side of the building, so they may not be completely off the grid...

She seriously doubted there was cell-phone service here.

As they pulled around behind the cabin and parked, Roger turned to her. "You are ten miles from the nearest house. Thirty miles from the closest grocery store. I strongly suggest you stay in the cabin and be a good girl."

"You have a gaming system in there, or Netflix?"

Roger gave her a disgusted snort and exited the vehicle. Lilly popped the lever on the side of the seat and climbed out after him. Then she looked around.

She actually liked the woods. When she'd been at the estate in New York, there'd been a huge expanse of forest she could wander through, but there had been carefully manicured paths to follow. These woods, she doubted she could even walk through. The trees were massive, and the under-brush was thick. There was a squirrel chittering at her on one of the branches, and she flipped it the bird. Man, it was cold, though. She pulled her jacket tighter around her. It was nice to be out in the bracing air, though. She'd been in that damn car for hours, looking at the back of his head and wishing she could wring his neck.

No doubt Mom would take care of that for her.

She smirked a little.

"What are you so happy about?"

Lilly started. She hadn't even heard him come up behind her. She shrugged it off and tilted her head at him. "Oh, just thinking what my mom is going to do to you when she gets her hands on you."

Roger's eyes narrowed, and he took a step closer to loom over her. "Your mother is never going to find you, here. They're chasing their tails in Virginia, looking for clues. By the time they figure out where we've been, we'll be gone again. Or rather, you will."

With that cryptic remark, he headed for the cabin.

Lilly was dying to pull the phone out and look for service, but she didn't dare. Not out in the open like this. Instead, she sent a heartfelt wish into the heavens that her mother was close.

HADEN DID A QUICK SCRUB DOWN, finding a few new sore places. Then he stepped out of the shower. Donna was waiting for him on the other side of the door, and they were going to crack some heads.

Haden winced at the thought. Donna never meant to be a weapon, that was just the way she'd turned out. And the Dogs didn't take advantage of her skills unless they absolutely had to. With one man down in the hospital, she had to step up to be their 4th in the fire team. She brought her very own unique set of skills, though, that he was very happy to have.

She was waiting for him when he stepped out. He dropped his bag outside the shower, and gave her a slight grin. "You ready to see what they know?"

Donna nodded. In the time he'd been in the shower, she'd braided her long hair down her back and secured it with a ponytail holder.

Haven loved seeing her hair down, but it was a distraction. Hell, the woman was a constant distraction. She made him want things. Things he'd not dared hope for for a long time.

Sometimes, he thought she might want them too. She just didn't know how to ask for them.

Dex had set one of the men up in a chair. It was the one that had recognized Donna. Donna crossed and rested a hand on the man's head, waking him instantly.

"Ah, you're awake," Haven said. "Excellent. Let's see what you know."

Haven grabbed a second chair, turning it to straddle in front of the man. He leaned his arms on top of the chair as he looked the man in the eye. "I thought I might give you a chance to talk before we moved on to other methods."

"Fuck you," the man said, stretching against his bonds.

Haven smiled. "Original. That must make you... a Marine."

The man's eyes flashed with anger, and Haven grinned even more. He glanced at Dex, standing to the side. "I think I got it in one."

Dex put a finger on his nose, grinning.

Haven looked at the former Marine. "So, were you active

duty when you volunteered to take the drug? Nah, you seem a little long in the tooth. A little too soft." He let his gaze wander down the man's body, resting on his paunch. "You must be a private contractor, in it for the money. Who do you work for? I think I know, but I just want confirmation."

The man smirked again, shaking his head. "You have no idea what you're in for."

Haven leaned forward, brows lifted. "Oh, really. Do tell..."

But the man clamped his mouth shut.

Haven's smile faded, replaced by a steely resolve. He leaned back in his chair, his gaze unwavering. "You think you can play tough, huh? Keep your secrets to yourself? Well, let me make one thing clear. We're not the ones you should be worried about."

The man's eyes narrowed, but he remained silent.

Haven continued, his voice low and intense. "You see, we have ways of finding out what we need to know. And trust me, we've dealt with people like you before. You may think you're invincible, but you're just a pawn in a much larger game. So, I suggest you start talking, because the consequences of silence won't be pleasant."

The man's defiance wavered for a moment, the fear in his eyes briefly surfacing. But then his expression hardened once again, and he spat out, "I'd rather die than betray my team."

Haven's jaw clenched, his patience wearing thin. "This isn't about betrayal or loyalty anymore. Lives are at stake. Innocent lives. And if you refuse to provide the information we need, you'll be responsible for the consequences."

Dex stepped forward, the air around him crackling with an unspoken threat. "You don't understand, buddy. We won't hesitate to do whatever it takes to protect those who can't protect themselves."

The man seemed to hesitate, a flicker of doubt crossing

his face. But then a stubborn determination settled in, and he remained silent.

Haven sighed, exchanging a glance with Dex. "Looks like we'll have to do this the hard way."

Donna stepped around the bed and into the man's sight. His gaze flickered and his face paled, a muscle twitching in his jaw.

"So, that reaction tells me you know who I am," Donna murmured, stepping toward him.

"Yeah, you're the cold bitch who killed my team."

Donna's dark brows went up over her eyes. "I've killed a few rogues," she admitted, "but I don't recognize you."

"Yeah, I'm not surprised," the man snarled, leaning forward. "You came through and did your brain touch, and my entire team was split. Only two of them made it through your test, and the rest of us were just cannon fodder. That's what he called us as he gave us the drug. They knew it wasn't going to work, but they did it anyway."

The Marine shook his head, and Haven thought he was more pissed at himself than at Donna. "That's not her fault," he murmured.

The man looked at him, snorting. "Right. Like she didn't know exactly what she was doing."

"I was as much of a prisoner at that time as you were," Donna said softly, and Haven glanced at her. That was the first time he'd ever heard her defend herself at all.

The man in the chair scoffed. "Right. I could tell by the way you moved through us so fast, ticking us off like we were items on a list."

Donna shook her head. "It doesn't matter now. Who hired you to attack us?"

The man once again clamped his mouth shut. Donna moved forward and panic flared in his watery blue eyes. "Hold on, hold on, hold on! Wait!"

Donna went still, hands hovering in the air.

"How do I know you won't kill me anyway?" the man asked, his jaw tight.

"You don't," Donna and Haven said together.

The man glanced between them, his mouth working. "It's some woman."

Haven frowned, glancing at Donna. She shook her head slightly, but he could feel her surprise as well.

"What woman?"

The man glanced to the side, and Haven could tell that he was trying to come up with a lie. Donna understood what he was doing as well. Without giving him a chance to protest, she stepped forward and rested her hand on the man's head.

"This is Gregorio Lane, or Greg. He has the minor ability to see connections. Where a person is going to be at a certain time, or when a vehicle is going to go through an underpass." She gave Haven a significant look. "He's not sure what the woman's name is, but they call her Grandmother. He's never seen her, only dealt with her 'captain', a man named Dante Vincent." She paused, her brow furrowing. "From what I can tell, they're trying to take over Hall's enterprise."

Haven frowned. That wasn't a lot of information. "Greg doesn't know who she is?"

Donna shook her dark head. "He just knows that all of their orders come down from her, through Vincent."

Donna frowned, stepping a little closer to the man. "He struggles because he knows he's not as good as the others. He was part of a group about three years ago that got a dose, but he's not sure what it was. Most of the group are dead. One of them he had to put down himself. They all worked for this woman, and have worked for her for three years. He has no idea who she is, but one of his guys thinks she's related to former Senator Hall. A sister or something. Vincent has a very tight mind. Nothing leaks from him." She paused, shaking her head slightly. "Vincent was in the military several years ago, and is much stronger than Greg. And our buddy here," she patted his cheek with her other hand, "has been trying to undermine Vincent, because he's such a dickhead."

Haven snorted. Of course, Vincent was a dickhead. "What do they want from us? Why are they following us?"

Donna frowned, her eyes moving beneath her lids as if she were actually scanning words on a page. She stopped suddenly, and her mouth fell open.

That couldn't be good.

Haven watched her scan the man for a few more seconds, then she blinked her eyes open and looked at him. "There's a bounty on my head," she said, her voice outraged.

Haven had suspected for a long time that there would be some kind of reward for her, but he hadn't wanted to voice it. Krammer had come across information months ago on the dark web about a reward just for information about Donna. It had been in a mercenary chat room, and it had been very clear who they had been talking about. He hadn't told Donna about it because he hadn't thought she needed to know. The woman didn't leave the building, so she was protected at all times.

Haven was pissed at himself, because he'd allowed her to insert herself into the investigation to find Lilly, and now they were both in an astronomical amount of danger.

"You aren't surprised," she murmured.

Haven shook his head. "We had intel a few months ago that someone was ramping up their efforts to find you."

Her head jerked forward in surprise. "And you didn't tell me?"

Wincing, he shook his head one time. "We thought it would stress you out more than you already were. You were under twenty-four hour guard and in an impenetrable building. There was no chance of you leaving. At least, not until Roger took Lilly."

She shook her head, her hands on her hips, and he could feel the anger radiating off her. "I should have been told. You don't have the right to treat me like a prisoner, withholding information like that."

Haven took a deep breath. "You're right. We should have told you, so you'd be aware. I apologize, Donna."

That seemed to smooth her feathers, but Haven didn't like feeling like he'd let her down. It had become very important to him that they only lift her up. He was disappointed in himself that he didn't give her the respect that she was so desperately fighting for.

She waved a hand at Greg. "I nulled his ability. He's normal, now, but I don't know what you want to do with him."

Haven wasn't sure either. Maybe he would turn him over to Officer Rose to deal with. Surely the CIA would like some insight into a shadow organization wreaking havoc and being a possible danger to national security? He texted a message to Wulfe asking him what he thought. Almost immediately, he got a thumbs up and a promise to call him in.

"Cuff him up and let's get the other guy in the chair."

Dex removed Greg from the chair and dropped him on the floor near the window. Then he grabbed the second guy, who was still out cold, and manhandled him into the chair. He wasn't as big as Greg, but it took some effort for Dex to get him there. As soon as he was slumped on the seat, Donna reached out a hand to rest on the man's head. He jerked awake with a start, slowly straightening. He glanced around the room, but didn't say a word.

"Greg says your name is Stafford. Is that right?"

There was no response, the guy's dark eyes unwavering as he stared at them.

"Greg says you're a useless bitch and he's tired of carrying your ass all across the country," Donna said, arms crossed and hip cocked as she looked him up and down.

The man's face rippled with anger, but he didn't say anything. Huffing at the guy's obstinance, Donna stepped forward and clapped her hand on the man's head.

She scanned him for several long seconds, her eyes moving quickly beneath her lids. Haven watched her face, amazed at what she could do.

When Dr. Shu created his formula, he went through so many different variations. He wrote down most of what he changed, but as Dr. Cole went through his journals, she realized that he had changed things that were not marked down. It was obvious to Haven that Donna had received a variation that was incredibly strong. She was, quite literally, the strongest telepath he'd ever seen. Well, the original three Dogs of War were strong, but her ability edged them out a little, he thought. A sense of pride rolled through him as he watched her work, and he wondered if there was anyone else as strong as her in the world. He sincerely hoped there wasn't.

Donna blinked her eyes open, and looked at Haven. "Mr. Stafford, here, is the brains of the operation. Every move Greg made, it was at his urging. He would *finesse* him to agree." She nodded her chin at the man in the chair, who was looking up at her in fear, now. She'd read him like a cheap paper, and he realized how very powerless he was. "They were supposed to retrieve me at all costs, even though their back-up didn't show."

Haven blinked. "How the fuck did they know where you were going to be?"

"They have a merc who sees things. He saw us at the hotel, and the direction we were heading. Then, with Greg's little knack at chance, they knew where to run into us. No pun," she murmured, huffing slightly.

Haven stood up and paced across the room. The chances of them doing exactly what she was suggesting... the odds of them being right had to be astronomical. Right? "Is that all they saw?"

Donna looked back at the man in the chair. He squeezed his eyes shut, as if to avoid her gaze, but it didn't matter. Donna clasped his head in both hands, her fingers going white with tension. Stafford cried out, but she didn't stop. "Vincent just sent orders to go to a pick-up across the state line if they failed to get me here. There's a cabin... I am the primary target. But they would have settled for taking the girl, knowing they could use her for leverage. They're supposed to get her tomorrow."

Donna jerked back from the man in the chair, her eyes going wide. She looked at Haven. "They were going to kill my daughter once they took me into custody."

Haven reached for her hands. "Donna, stop. They don't have you, so they have to keep Lilly alive right now. And even if they take you, I doubt they would kill your kid. That would remove all of their leverage over you."

She shook her head, her dark eyes dazed, but she held onto his hands. Haven left his shields down so that she could feel how much he believed what he told her, and that seemed to calm her down. "Hey, look at me." Moving closer, he cupped her cheeks in his hands. "Don't let him shake you. Find out where that damn cabin is. Because Lilly needs you."

She nodded in his hold, and turned toward their prisoner. Mr. Stafford was out of it, barely conscious. His eyes widened when he saw her approaching, though, and he tried to move away. Donna wouldn't let him. She latched onto his head with both hands, and Haven had no doubt that she would find the exact information they needed.

He glanced up, meeting Dex's eyes. Haven could feel the anxiety rolling off the other man, but he didn't move to intervene. And he didn't say anything. They were in a dire situation, and they had the power to change the course of their lives. To save lives. So they were going to do what they needed to do.

Donna winced, and tilted her head, like she was trying to look at something. "Somebody pull up a map on your phone," she murmured.

Haven reached in his pocket and pulled up Google maps.

"I think they're in Georgia, but I need to look... ," she murmured, eyes still closed. "They're on a lake, kind of."

Haven used his fingers to zoom into Georgia, then he held the phone out to Donna. She opened her eyes and blinked, but kept her hands on Stafford's head. He held the phone out, but she shook her head. "No, I'm looking at it upside down. Turn the phone around to face you, hold it like normal."

Then she peered over the edge. "Zoom in on that. I think it's up there by the South Carolina state line."

Haven used his fingers to zoom in. Donna closed her eyes for a second, then looked back down at the map. "There's a town nearby that starts with Hart."

Haven zoomed in. Hartwell, Georgia was not very big, but it looked like it catered to Hartwell Lake, which looked massive. It covered the South Carolina border on the south west side, and it appeared to have hundreds of little finger inlets, all around the lake. Haven zoomed in even closer, still holding the phone toward Donna. She waved a finger over one area. "I feel like it's in there."

Haven took a screenshot of the map, then shared it with his people and Aiden.

*I'll see if I can get satellite images*, Krammer texted back.

Donna was beginning to sag, and he knew filtering

through all the little pieces of information in Stafford's brain had worn her out.

"Donna, I think we have enough, for now."

She frowned, her eyes closed again, as she continued to hold the merc's head in her hands. After a few seconds, she blinked her eyes open. "I think I've got everything he knew about what they were doing. Vincent isn't very far away, though. He was supposed to meet them down there for the exchange."

"Great. So, we have two separate assholes to deal with now."

"Yes," she agreed, her voice tired. "But at least we know they both have the same goal. Snatching me." She shook her head as she let Stafford go. The man slumped in the chair, and for a minute Haven worried that she'd killed him.

"I didn't," she murmured, honing in on his thoughts without any apparent effort. Or maybe he was just broadcasting. "Though I wanted to. I stripped him of his abilities. He did have more information about what the Grandmother had planned, so I suggest you get Rose on a plane to take custody of them."

Haven nodded. "I already messaged Wulfe. He'll get him down here."

Donna moved toward the door. "We should think about moving soon. I don't know what Vincent can do, but I have a feeling we won't like it."

"We will," he promised, moving toward her. "Why don't you go lie down for a while. As soon as we can turn these jokers over to Rose, or one of his flunkies, we'll go check on Jibari and get out of here. We have an appointment in Georgia."

A flash of a smile slipped over her lips, and she leaned toward him. Haven wrapped his arms around her in a gentle hug, pressing a kiss to the top of her head. "Go lie down. I'll wake you in a bit."

He watched as she crossed to the bed. She curled up on her side and was asleep almost instantly. Gently, he pulled the comforter over top of her, fighting the urge to crawl into bed with her. Turning away, he returned to the other room. Until they handed over their prisoners, they needed to stay alert.

**14**

Less than two hours later, CIA Officer Kevin Rose arrived in person with three other spooks to take the mercs into custody. He looked at them, passed out on the floor, and gave Haven a look. Haven merely shrugged, grinning slightly.

Kevin was not a bad guy, and Haven liked him for the most part. But Kevin's first obligation was to the CIA, no matter what the collateral damage. Haven knew that if his bosses deemed it necessary to take Donna into custody, or any of them for that matter, he would do it, or die trying. He was a company man through and through.

In that vein, he didn't like being at the beck and call of a mere former Army Ranger. Haven tried not to be smug, because a little over a year ago Kevin had been running the show in the New York takedown. And he'd seen Haven at his worst. But that had been before Donna had started working with him.

Man, what a crazy trip that had been. Noah still teased him about the fucking zebra he'd created as a distraction to get them off his tail. He'd actually created the specter deliberately, because he knew that Donna would more than likely pick up on the energy expenditure. And she had.

He could play nice for a little while. He held out a hand to the other man. "Thanks for taking these guys off my hands. We need to check on Jibari, but I didn't want to stretch our team too thin."

"Agreed," Rose said, bracing his arms behind his back. "The Dog Pound is running light as well right now, isn't it?"

Haven fought not to react. Yes, technically the CIA was one of their allies, but they didn't need to know information about critical security. Shrugging lightly, he made a 'meh' motion, and turned away. "I'm going to go get Donna up. Dex, in the car in five."

"Roger that," Dex said, already moving to pick up what he needed to in the room.

Haven knocked lightly on the adjoining door. Donna answered it almost immediately, and he knew she'd heard Rose arrive. Haven stepped toward her, and she eased the door open enough that he could slip through. "Maybe if I wait here long enough he'll disappear," he whispered, grinning.

Donna grinned as well, her arms folded under her breasts. She was still completely dressed, but she seemed a little refreshed. Apparently the cat nap had done her well.

"I thought you were friends," she said.

Haven gave her a look. "Being friends with the CIA is like trying to keep a shark on a leash. Theoretically, they'd be a good ally, but if they turn on you, you're done."

Donna snorted as she went for her bag. "Yes, I can see that. Shouldn't you make nice with him then?"

Haven shrugged, watching her move. "I'd rather be a little abrupt getting away from him then give him any information he can use against us later."

She nodded, slipping into the bathroom to retrieve her

dirty clothes. She stuffed them into the bag, zipped it up and turned to him. "I think he's gone now. And I'm ready."

Haven glanced around, appreciating how efficient she was. "Okay. Let's go."

~

DR. ELIZABETH COLE smiled when they walked in the small hospital room, and stood to meet them. The woman looked like she should have been on a magazine cover, with her pale gray blouse and black slacks and heels. Her blond hair was up and away from her face in an elegant twist, and she wore flawless makeup. Black-rimmed glasses shielded her wide blue eyes, but Donna thought she wore them only because she wanted to look more scholarly.

Donna always felt self-conscious around Dr. Cole. The woman was beautiful, and well-bred, and effortlessly beautiful, but she was also stunningly intelligent. Donna wanted to hate her for what her ex-husband had done to them, but as bad as Damon Wilkes had been, Elizabeth seemed to be his opposite in every way. She fought for the men Dr. Shu had tested upon, and she'd done a mountain of good work. And she was one of the most intelligent doctors she'd ever met or worked with.

Dr. Cole moved around the foot of Jibari's bed to give her a hug. Donna wasn't wild about physical touch, but she'd gotten used to it from the woman. Her shields were also not especially strong, which allowed Donna to sense the woman's genuine care for her, and her relief that they were unharmed. Dr. Cole was doing her best in a difficult situation. As they all were.

Donna pulled back and looked at Jibari. The tall man took up most of the length of the bed, but he was motionless. When she brushed against his mind, it was dark.

Dr. Cole was hugging Haven, and murmuring a few words to him. Haven nodded a couple of times, then turned to look at his teammate. Donna saw the exact second when he realized that Jibari was truly unconscious, and unable to speak to them.

"Is he sedated," she asked.

Dr. Cole nodded. "A few things showed up on his brain scan, and I wanted to put him under until you could get here. What do you feel, or see?"

Donna frowned, gently probing again. "Blackness. And quiet."

"There was a significant brain bleed from the crash. He has a significant intracranial hematoma. I've given him meds to slow the bleeding, but I'm going to have to repair the bleed. I wanted to get your take on his state before I did anything. The surgery is risky, and I would prefer not to do it if I didn't have to." She glanced around the room. "I'm not even sure I would get the surgical support here I need. If I have to move him to a trauma center, it may not go well."

Donna appreciated that Dr. Cole had waited for her evaluation. It was one of the skills she'd been practicing, and wanted to build on. It was very easy for her to read a mind, whether it wanted to be read or not. It was more challenging to try to enact physical change. It took power, and knowledge, and subtle manipulations of energy to encourage the body to respond to her prodding. Donna was very glad she'd had the chance to lay down for a couple of hours, because it was also very physically taxing.

The risk was worth the reward, though. Jibari was a vital part of the team, and if she could repair any part of what had been damaged in the crash, she would.

"Are you sure there's no other way," Haven asked the doctor. "Donna is already drained from interrogating the mercs that hit us."

Dr. Cole shrugged lightly. "I'm willing to do surgery to relieve the pressure on the brain, but it's risky in the best of environments, let alone in a place like this."

Haven glanced around. The hospital was tiny, and the staff probably wasn't used to dealing with a lot of traumas. He looked at Jibari. If the man was awake, he would be pushing them away. He would never want to risk the team for his health. Haven knew they would need him, though.

Donna read all the thoughts as they rolled across Haven's public mind, then he met her eyes. "It's up to you," he said. "You know we'll take care of you."

Donna gave a single nod, and moved toward the bed. There was no question of what she would do, only how much it might damage her.

HAVEN DIDN'T like Donna putting herself in danger again, but he trusted in her abilities. She was an amazing nurse, and he thought she knew her own limits. When she was scanning a patient, she would pull away if she needed to. He'd seen her do it more than once. He'd also seen what she'd been capable of doing. When Aiden's wife Angela had been carrying baby Fallon, a pall had hung over the building. There were complications. First with nausea and iron issues, then high blood pressure and pre-eclampsia. Dr. Cole had been at a loss, and she'd hired a special OB doctor to come in for Angela's care. The OB had been grim after the initial consultation, explaining that the pre-eclampsia would not be resolved until the baby was born.

Then Donna had started having sessions with her. She would lay her hands on Angela's distended belly, and the tension in the young mother's face would ease. Haven had seen her do it several times. Baby Fallon had been born perfectly healthy less than a month later, with no sign of complications.

The special OB that Dr. Cole had hired had merely shaken his head, unable to articulate how Angela and the baby had pulled out of the danger they were in.

But Haven had seen the way the sessions had drained Donna. She would walk out of the room fine, but as soon as she was out of sight, her body would almost melt to the floor. More than once he'd helped her back to her rooms, and left her sleeping, exhausted. Haven had understood her motivation, though. At the time the men still looked at her as if she were Belladonna, the woman they'd all seen working for Dr. Shu. They were leery of letting her help them. It had only been after the baby had been born, and word had gotten out that Donna had helped them, that the men had started to accept her.

Haven had faith that Donna could help Jibari. He just didn't want her to hurt herself doing it. So, he stood near the bed, watching yet again as she fought for one of the people he cared about at the detriment to herself.

IT TOOK a whole day before Lilly got a chance to use her phone. Roger didn't seem to care if she went outside, but he watched her like a damned hawk, and if she disappeared from his sight, he was there to scold her and threaten to zip-tie her.

"I thought you said there was no one around here? So why are you worried?" she snapped.

The man had crossed his arms over his big chest. "You're my paycheck. If you get lost in the woods and eaten by a bear, I'm going to be very angry."

The bear comment had given her pause. Were there bears

out here? It was wooded enough there probably could be. If she had some idea where they were maybe she would know if there were bears. North Carolina definitely had them, but she knew they were farther south than that. Did South Carolina or Georgia have them? Did she have bear facts floating around in her brain like that? No. So, maybe it didn't matter if she knew. Other than to tell Mom if she could get a text message out.

"Can I walk down to the water?" she asked.

Roger looked from her to the distant glimmer of water. It was at least half a mile away, but within sight of the cabin. "Yes, but I had better be able to look out and see you at all times. If I don't, I'm dragging you back to the cabin and securing you, and you won't leave it again. Do you understand?"

Lilly saluted him, and turned to walk toward the water. It took her more than half an hour to get there, but once she got to the beach, she smiled. It was beautiful. The water was dark in the deeper parts, but she could see fish swimming in the shallower parts. It was only as she was standing at the edge of the water when she realized this may not just be a pond. The shoreline went on and on, calling to her to explore it, but she glanced back at the cabin. If Roger saw her disappear down the shore she had no doubt he would come after her. She had no desire to be trapped in the silent cabin with him any longer.

If this was a lake, maybe there would be boaters, or people in canoes or something. Maybe she would be able to wave someone down. No, it was winter time. She doubted anyone was swimming in this coldness.

Did she have the right to pull people into her danger, though, even if she did see a boater? The thought of someone getting hurt or killed for her made her sick. She would try to send Mom a message, then maybe she would just stay down here for a while. If she happened to see someone, she would decide then whether or not to wave them down.

Glancing back at the cabin, she saw Roger standing there. She flipped him the bird with both hands, then turned and faced the water, dropping to her butt on the beach. She knew exactly where he was, so it was a good time to try to text Mom. She pulled her phone from her sock and powered it up. Only twenty-five percent battery. She had no power cord with her, so she went to the text screen. Her heart leapt into her throat as she saw a message from her mother.

*Noted. Stay safe however you can, baby! I love you. Message when you can.*

Just those few sentences were enough to give her heart. Mom was looking for her, and she would find her.

*Mom, I love you too. I'm ok right now. Deep in woods some-where. Not sure where. Might be near a lake. He warned me there were bears, but dk if he's joking or not. Battery is dying, so I may not be able to text again. I think he's giving me to someone soon, or selling me or smtg. He's waiting on someone to contact him. I'll leave phone on so you can hopefully track it. Love you.*

She hit the send button, then looked out over the water. There was a scuff on the rocks, and she suddenly knew that Roger was behind her. What had taken her half an hour to traverse had taken him mere minutes. As surreptitiously as she could, she shoved the phone into the sand beneath her butt, praying that her mother didn't respond. She thought it was still on silent, but she hadn't checked it.

Turning her head, she leaned against her propped knees, looking back at him. "I haven't moved since I flipped you the bird, asshole. You saw me sit down."

She poured on the bitchiness, giving him a disgusted look. Roger loomed over her. "What do you have in your hand? You were looking at something."

Luckily, she'd found a feather that some bird had lost at

the water's edge. It had piqued her interest, so she'd grabbed it. She held it up for him to see. "I was trying to figure out what kind of bird this was from, if you must know."

Roger looked at the feather, then her face. She held his gaze with her own, knowing that she had to appear to be a spoiled little brat to pull this off. Eventually, he glanced toward the water. Lilly could tell he was pissed that he hadn't caught her doing something. "Let's go," he said, waving a hand at her to get up. "I need to run to town to get some food, and you're not staying out here."

"I just got here," she wailed, praying that she'd pushed the phone deep enough into the dirt and sand that he wouldn't see it. She pushed to her feet, surreptitiously glancing at where she'd sat. She could see the tiniest of bumps she thought might be the topmost corner, but everything seemed to be covered. No glint of black. She huffed as she walked past him, tempted to nail him in the gut a good one, but that would only piss him off.

Roger shoved her shoulder as he fell in behind her. "You're getting awfully used to being mouthy. I suggest you shut it."

Lilly tromped through the brush toward the cabin, arms crossed over her chest. As soon as they were back at the cabin, he shoved her inside the door. Before she could turn around he had grabbed her wrists and secured them behind her back. Lilly cried out, because he hadn't been nice about it. Then he shoved her down to the couch. Before she could do anything, he'd knelt before her and was securing her ankles, as well. Lilly was furious that she couldn't move, but she didn't fight him, just because she didn't want him to tighten them any further. She glared at him, though, and dreamt of ways to get back at him. "You're an asshole," she said softly, "and you're going to die."

Before she could blink, he punched her in the jaw. There was incredible pain, then everything went dark.

DONNA WAS SWIMMING in the depths of Jibari's mind, doing what she could to minimize the bleeding, when there was a shock to her system. At first, she'd thought it was Jibari, responding to something she'd done. But he'd jerked as well. Her eyes blinked open, and she looked at Haven. "Did you call me?"

Haven shook his head. "I know not to disturb you."

"How long have I been under with him?"

"About forty minutes," Dr. Cole said, glancing at the clock on the wall. "And whatever you're doing seems to be working. He's calming, and his blood pressure seems to be settling."

Donna glanced around, feeling out of sorts in spite of what Dr. Cole told her. Yes, it was good news, but something had jerked her out of her healing trance. What had it been? The unmistakeable sound of her phone pinging rang through the room. She reached for the bedside table, where she'd set it, and swiped it on. Then she read the message with her heart in her throat. Lilly was okay. For the moment, at least.

Haven's phone went off as well, and he knew it was probably Krammer, following up. "Do we have a location?" He listened for a moment, then something flared in his gaze. He nodded at her. "Send it to me."

Moving toward her, he dropped his phone in his pocket. "We have a triangulation point. It's a rough guesstimate, but we're hoping that we'll get better intel by the time we get there. And we can cross it with Stafford's instructions."

"Let's go," a rough voice said, and they all turned toward the bed.

Jibari blinked at them and one side of his mouth tilted up slightly. He gave Haven a thumbs-up, and Haven moved toward his friend, taking his hand. Jibari wasn't as strong as he normally was, but Haven was so glad to see his buddy awake that he didn't care. "You're going to sit this one out, my friend."

The African sat up in his bed, weaving a little, and tried to swing his legs to the side.

"Whoa, whoa, whoa," Dr. Cole cried, pressing on his shoulders. "You are not getting out of this bed until I check you out. I don't care how good you feel."

Haven agreed with the doctor. No matter what Donna had done for him, Jibari was very obviously not ready to go on the hunt for a kidnapper. Haven would feel better about leaving him behind, though, now that he was conscious. He kept that thought tight under his shield, because he didn't want his teammate to feel slighted. "We're going to need you to come get us when we find Lilly. You need to recover here, as long as you can, and come along later. Do you understand?"

"I am willing to fight," he protested.

Haven knew his heart was willing, but his body was not. "I know you are, my friend, but I need you to get Dr. Cole out of here safely, once she releases you."

Jibari scowled, but his head dropped back to the bed, as though he couldn't hold it up any longer. Finally, he nodded, his lips pursed. His dark gaze drifted to Donna, and he held out his hand. "I felt you, there, doing wicked things in my brain. But I thank you."

Donna took his arm in her own, clasping it tightly, before she let him go. "Rest. Take a nap. We're hours, possibly days, away from rescuing Lilly, so take some time to recover. I'm sure the doctor has a few more tests for you to do before she feels comfortable letting you go."

Jibari gave the slightest nod, before his eyes drifted shut.

With a pointed look, Dr. Cole led them out of the hospital room. Once the door was closed behind them, she leaned close. "He's nowhere near ready to go anywhere. Do you think you got the bleeding stopped?"

Donna nodded, arms crossed over her stomach. "It is stopped, and I was guiding the repair. I've kicked his system into overdrive to repair itself. He's going to need nutrients, and rest. If he gets out of bed too soon, he will undo all of the work I just did."

Dr. Cole nodded. "Maybe I'll slip a little sedative into his next IV."

Donna nodded, her shoulders sagging. Haven reached out and rested a hand on her shoulder, trying to feed her some of his own energy. They couldn't do that, of course, but he could let her know he was supporting her, no matter what. "We have a date with a dead man," he told Dr. Cole, and some light entered Donna's dark eyes.

"We do," she agreed, smiling slightly. Roger McCullough had been a pain in all their asses for too long, and it was time for him to pay.

## 15

Haven knew how tired Donna was, but they couldn't stop. As they loaded into the helicopter that had delivered Dr. Cole from Virginia, Haven made sure to keep a hand on her at all times. She was weaving on her feet, and he didn't want her to fall and hurt herself. Copper reached out a hand and helped her inside, and Dex helped her strap in. The men knew what she'd done for Jibari, and they were showing her how they could that they appreciated her.

Haven settled next to her on the seat and strapped in, then he gave the pilot the landing coordinates. Krammer had found them an area nearby that would accommodate the chopper, yet keep them out of sight of the cabin where McCullough had Lilly. They'd have to hike about a half mile into the woods to find it, but they were up to the challenge. He would carry Donna if he needed to.

As they lifted into the air, the gravitational pull seemed to make Donna's head weave. Without thought, he reached out, unsnapped the belt and lifted her into his arms, nestling her head against the hollow of his shoulder. With a sigh, she settled across his lap, and sagged into his body. It was a challenge keeping his body from responding to her nearness, but the closeness and the trust she was giving him was more important than any physical enjoyment. Haven would hold her exactly like this for as long as the flight was, and be thrilled about it. Because she would need her energy to find Lilly and fight McCullough. They would be there with her, of course, but he knew for a fact she wanted to deal with him herself. And she deserved to be able to do that. McCullough had been a thorn in their side for too long.

They flew for almost forty minutes, the sun leaving a blazing trail to their right. It was going to be darker than hell, soon, and if they went after McCullough in the dark, it was going to be that much harder to fight him. Personally, Haven thought it would be a good idea to hole up somewhere for a few hours, then go in early in the morning, in the wee hours of dawn. Haven felt his phone buzz in his pocket, but he wasn't going to move. He had a delicious arm-full of woman, and he wasn't going to give it up.

*Krammer found us a cabin nearby*, Dex said. *Three miles from the target.*

*Excellent*, Haven said. *I'm not sure we can take her in this exhausted.*

*I'm fine*, Donna said, though she didn't move from his hold or even open her eyes.

Both men startled, and looked at each other in surprise. No one had ever intercepted their telepathic conversations before.

*I don't think that's a great idea, Donna*, Haven told her, rolling with the unexpected interruption. *We know he's not going to move tonight. I think we should get some sleep and set out early in the morning, before they've had a chance to get up.*

He could feel her resistance, but also her eventual acceptance. She'd overtaxed herself today, first with the crash, then the interrogations, then with helping Jibari, and she recognized that she wasn't at peak performance. *Fine, but just for a few hours.*

*That's fine*, Haven agreed. *Go back to sleep.*

Her mind disappeared almost immediately. He glanced at Dex. *As soon as we land, take point. If McCullough is any good at all, three miles may be too close.*

Dex nodded, checking his gear. Then he tilted his head back against the seat and closed his eyes. Copper was already out, and completely missed the conversation.

It was odd just being the three of them. This was the first time any of them had been seriously injured on a job. Well, Copper had been shot a time or two, but he'd gone on and continued the mission with the team. Working without Jibari felt like they were missing a limb. He was where he needed to be, though, and Haven knew he would bust his ass to get out here as soon as he possibly could.

Twenty minutes later they landed in a small grassy field. Dex immediately leapt out and started canvassing the area at a jog. Haven helped Donna down out of the chopper, and kept a hold on her waist as the rotor wash died down. The chopper itself would stay here, and the pilot would stay inside, so that they had immediate transportation if they needed it.

The cabin they would be using was to the east, Krammer informed them, almost a half-mile through the woods. Haven didn't mind the hike. It gave him a chance to stretch his legs. Donna eventually woke enough that she could ambulate on her own. They arrived at the rental cabin just as the moon crested above the trees.

Dex came out of the cabin and waited for them on the porch. "Fire's lit and the water heater is on. There's some canned food in the cupboards if you're hungry. Only two beds in the main room, but they look comfortable."

"Donna, go crash," Haven said, and she didn't even argue. "Dex, you go crash, too. Copper and I will keep watch."

Dex gave a salute, and headed back inside. Haven went inside long enough to make sure Donna was secure and covered with a blanket, then he looked for something to snack on. He grabbed a bag of pretzels and a bottle of water, and returned to the front porch. Copper was out doing a circuit around the cabin. Haven knew he'd probably find a tree to park under, and keep watch.

He glanced at the luminous dial of his watch. It was just past 8pm. They would get a few hours of sleep in, then head toward the cabin where they thought Lilly was. Once they got there they would decide if they needed to rush the cabin or stake it out in an ambush. Whichever plan would keep Lilly the safest. If anything happened to her, there was no force on Earth that could stop Donna from destroying McCullough. Kevin Rose had made it clear that they wanted the former Secret Service operative alive if possible. Haven didn't promise him anything.

There was a very strong possibility that Donna would take matters into her own hands, and he wasn't sure he would blame her.

IT WAS nighttime when McCullough finally returned, and Lilly was pissed. She needed to pee, and there was no way she could do it trussed up like a chicken. Her jaw throbbed where he'd punched her, and she thought some of her teeth might be loose.

Roger McCullough was going to die, if not at her mother's hands, then at her own.

She glared at him as he walked in the door, and he chuckled at her. "What, princess? No smart mouth?"

"If you don't want me to piss this couch, asshole, you'd better let me go to the bathroom."

Roger snorted, and continued into the kitchen area. With her luck, he'd leave her here just to prove what a dick he was. Eventually, he returned, and pulled out the knife he kept tucked into the corner of his jeans pocket. Cutting the black zip-ties, he gave her a look. "Don't be stupid and get yourself dead."

Lilly couldn't help but roll her eyes. "Right. You can't kill me. I'm the ticket to your payday."

"No," he corrected, his eyes hard. "Your mother is. Remember that."

Lilly held his gaze for a second, then pushed away from him and got up. She crossed to the tiny bathroom, wishing she still had her phone on her. It gave her a sense of security, if nothing else. She used the bathroom, and headed back out into the cabin. It was just a single large room, with a bathroom snugged into one corner and the kitchen area in the opposite corner. There was a couch and chair in front of a fireplace, and a set of bunkbeds on the far wall. It wasn't big, by any means.

"If you're hungry you can eat a can of soup," he said, dropping down into the chair with a steaming cup in his hands.

She hadn't eaten anything all day, so she very gladly went into the kitchen nook and chose a can of broccoli soup from the shelf. She poured it into a mug like he had and put it in the ancient microwave on the counter. It took almost four minutes to get warm, but she didn't care. As soon as it was bubbling on the edges, she took it out.

Lilly hated to even think she was eating with him, so she took her mug out onto the front porch, closed the door and sat on the step to eat her soup. If she could have gone farther, she would have, but he would just bitch at her. As she ate, she listened to the sounds of the woods around her. The dirt man would probably love it out here, even though there weren't a lot of flowers. It was mostly trees, and prickly grass. The sun had gone down, and there was the slightest blush of light on the horizon. Then it faded away. It was a beautiful night.

She cocked her head. Was that the sound of a helicopter? Her heart raced as she thought about running out into the field to wave it down, praying it could even see her in the dark. Maybe they had tracked her cell phone from the last message she sent. Was Mom almost here?

The door opened behind her, and the asshole came out. He looked up at the sky as well, and Lilly felt like she needed to distract him. "Who are you selling me to?" she demanded.

She scraped the soup down in her cup, the spoon clanging on the side of the porcelain. Then she slurped the last of the soup from the cup.

Roger glared at her, and she knew he was pissed at her. She didn't care.

"It doesn't matter," he told her, then went back inside, slamming the door behind himself.

Lilly huffed, glad that she'd distracted him enough to not pay the helicopter any attention. He may have just been checking on her whereabouts, too. Couldn't let the golden goose wander away.

Lilly tried to plan out what she'd do if it was a rescue attempt. Should she try to tackle him? Or just get the fuck out of there? If they were honing in on her location, maybe she should run down to the beach where she'd sent the message from? No, she had a feeling that if Mom got close, it didn't matter what she did.

Her throat tightened as she thought about seeing her mother again, and feeling her arms wrap around her. She'd gotten used to having her hugs over the past year, and she craved them now. Quite desperately. She was also worried about Tini. And Asher. McCullough hadn't said exactly what he'd done to them. She'd just left with him in the hopes that he would leave them alone. If he had really hurt them...

Lilly stoked her anger. Sadness wasn't doing her any favors. Anger would keep her focused. Should she go to bed in the hopes that something would happen sooner? There was no way she could sleep right now. She wished for her laptop, so she could read the stories she was following. She snorted. If she had pen and paper, she would write her own story. Maybe with a romantic lead covered in potting soil...

# 16

When Lilly had eventually come in and gone to bed, Roger had seemed asleep in his chair, eyes closed and head tipped back against the cushion.

If she'd had a knife she would have tried to cut his throat.

She curled up on the cot and pulled the light blanket over top of herself. Sleep claimed her quickly, though she tried to listen for rescue.

Lilly was woken by rough hands pushing her to her face on the cot. Her hands were bound, and a nasty cloth was shoved into her mouth, making her gag.

"If you throw up you'll suffocate yourself," Roger said calmly, stepping away from her.

Lilly twisted her head, turning to glare at him in the meager light from the fire. But her eyes went wide with fear. There were six unfamiliar men standing in the cabin's shadows, besides Roger. They were dressed in semi-military gear, like the Dogs preferred to wear. Weapons decorated their vests, both knives and guns. And they all wore black camo masks and helmets, which sent a chill of fear through her.

They looked like a team of badasses, and her heart sank. Was this the team that was going to take her away? Roger had sold her, apparently, and this was what she was going to have to deal with.

Glancing toward the window, she tried to decide what time it was. Still dark outside. Even though she'd been excited, she'd fallen asleep for a while, so maybe early morning?

One of the men stepped out of the shadows. He was taller than the others, and he carried an AR15 like it was just a part of him. He wore no mask or helmet, and his eyes made her shiver. They were a pale color she thought might be pretty in the light, but they were cold and distant. "It's a pleasure to meet you, Lilly. I'm Dante Vincent. I have a feeling we're going to be very good friends." His mouth tilted up slightly, but it was crooked. There was a gnarly scar that ran down from the edge of his mouth, across his jawline, and down over his neck. She wished whoever had tried to kill the man had done a better job.

She glared, helplessly, as she watched the men leave the cabin. Even as a group, they moved almost silently, and for the first time she wished for some of the abilities her mother had. If she could just let them know they were walking into a trap. And that she was the bait.

After the group left, she glared at Roger. He chuckled, which made her even madder. "Oh, if you could see your expression, right now," he laughed. "What will really make you mad is knowing that we knew about your little messages with your mother. Did you really think I didn't know you still had your phone? We just needed to get to a place more conducive to taking her alive."

Lilly went still, and the blood rushed to her head as she thought about the messages she'd sent. She thought she'd been so sly, and sneaky. When in reality he'd just been playing her. "Asshole," she mumbled around her gag, and he laughed again.

Lilly wiggled at her bonds, but they were so tight.

"Don't bother," he murmured. "Now stand up. We're going to put you in the bathroom, just in case someone makes it through that front door."

He hoisted her up by her arm, and Lilly knew this would be the only chance she got to fight back at all. Bending down just a little, she slammed into him with her back, her hands grabbing for the tiniest of lifelines. Roger cursed and swung her around, and she thought her right arm was going to pop out of the socket. Fuck, that hurt. But she palmed the item, praying he didn't notice. Roger pretty much dragged her to the bathroom and tossed her inside, to the floor. Lilly stared daggers at him, but he only laughed. He must have been paid, already. That was why he was in such a good mood.

Roger left her in the bathroom, and she debated whether or not to use the knife she'd taken from the corner of his pocket. No, she would wait until she heard something going on outside. Then she would make her move.

HAVEN PUT out a call at three a.m. *Time to get ready.*

Dex rolled up in bed immediately. Donna sighed, stretching on the mattress. Then she sat up as well. Haven heard Copper coming in from the woods.

"What's the plan, boss man?" Dex murmured, voice raspy from sleep.

Haven folded his arms across his chest and planted his feet. "We're going to hike down there and get Lilly back. I sent Rose a message, and let him know we were moving in. He's on standby. We're to take McCullough alive." He looked directly at Donna, brows raised. She waved a negligent hand at him. "Only take him out if there is absolutely no recourse. He's a valuable target. Joint Task Force Omega and the CIA would like to have him in custody. He is a material witness. And as much of a pain in the ass as he's been, he's probably got a shitload of knowledge in that warped brain of his. Hell, he might even know about the Grandmother. Or Vincent. We need to at least question him."

Donna sighed, and he knew he'd gotten through to her. Although if Lilly was hurt, all bets would be off.

"Do what you need to do to wake up," he said. "We roll out in five. Donna, you're going to have to slide in as our fourth, taking Jibari's spot. Can you do that?"

She blinked, and nodded. "I'll watch your backs. At least until we get close. Then I'm going in and securing my daughter."

Yeah, he thought she'd do something like that. "Just remember that we're all here to get her back. Don't try to take him on on your own. We don't know exactly what he's capable of. We need to work together to make sure she stays safe."

Donna nodded again, though her mouth went tight. It was smart to use the entire team, she just didn't like it.

Dex and Donna got dressed in their tactical vests, jackets and weapons. Copper had never taken his off. And neither had Haven. It was a part of him, almost, so he wore the rig all the time. Copper had a big AR slung over his shoulder.

Haven watched Donna strap her weapons holster on. Even in the midst of impending danger, he found her unbelievably attractive. Her hair was mussed from sleeping, but even as he watched, she twisted it into a tail, then piled it into bun. She made some twisting movement with her hands, and her hair was secured. One of these days he was going to take that hair down, and explore it at his leisure.

*You're drooling boss man*, Dex said in his head. *Tighten up.*

Haven glanced at his buddy, grinning slightly. *Roger that, Bad Dog Two.*

Heading out the door, he took a heavy breath. They were about to face an extremely dangerous opponent, and he needed to have his head in the game. Dex was right to tug him into line. Going down the steps, he took off into a jog. He glanced back a couple of times to make sure the rest of the team were keeping up, then continued on.

Krammer pinged him when they got within a mile of McCullough's cabin, and they slowed. It was time for stealth. Haven left the line open to their tech, so that he could hear and record what went on.

*Dex, take point. Try to confirm she's still there. We'll follow at a slower pace and secure a perimeter around the cabin.*

Dex headed into the night, swinging to the North. Haven watched him until he lost sight of him. The moon was weak tonight, which had its pros and cons. The lack of light would hide them. The lack of light would also hide anyone coming after them.

*Donna, do you feel anything?*

*No, not yet. Too far out of my range.*

They moved closer, until they were only about two hundred and fifty yards from where the cabin was supposed to be. The moon had ducked behind clouds, and the diffuse light was not enough to see shit. If there was a cabin in front of them, there were no lights lit inside.

*Just found Lilly's phone down on the beach. Still has a charge. I smell Roger and her from about six hours ago. Pretty sure they're still here, Bad Dog One.*

*Roger that,* Haven said, trying to see through the dark. Was that a glint of light on metal? Or maybe on a windshield?

Haven squinted into the darkness, his senses attuned to every subtle shift in the environment. The weight of Lilly's safety pressed on his shoulders, urging him to remain hypervigilant. The tension in the air was palpable, a collective breath held by the team as they zeroed in on their objective.

*Maintain your positions and keep your eyes peeled,* Haven whispered through their minds.

Dex's reply was a mere brush of acknowledgment, from somewhere up ahead. Donna's breathing came across the line, a steady rhythm as she waited for any indication of their next move. Copper's silence was a testament to his focus, a sentinel on watch.

As they closed in on the cabin's location, the murmur of the wind and the distant rustle of leaves conspired to hide their approach. The uncertainty of the situation gnawed at Haven, reminding him of the gravity of their mission. McCullough was no ordinary adversary, and Lilly's life hung in the balance.

Krammer's voice crackled through the open line in his earpiece. "I'm detecting faint movement in the vicinity. Proceed with caution."

Haven signaled the team to halt, his stance tense as he evaluated the situation. Every nerve was electrified, heightened awareness drowning out all else. A flicker of doubt raced through his mind—was the movement a sign of danger, or was it the movement of the night?

"Donna," Haven's voice was a breath against the comm, "any insights?"

A brief pause, then Donna's voice came back. "Still out of range. But I'm ready to move in as soon as you give the word."

Haven felt a mix of reassurance and concern. Donna's determination was admirable, but the unpredictable nature of their target demanded caution. It was a game, now. Whoever could get the drop first would win. And they needed to win.

The four of them maintained their positions, their senses

on high alert. The night seemed to stretch endlessly, the seconds ticking by with excruciating slowness.

A whisper of static buzzed in Haven's ear. *I've got visual on the cabin,* Dex murmured. *Lights are out, but it's there.*

Haven nodded to himself, his mind racing with considerations. *Maintain your position.*

Their strategy depended upon precision, on timing, on every element falling into place. Haven's gaze swept the surroundings, absorbing the details he could discern from the scant moonlight. The tension was a palpable force, wrapping around them as they stood on the edge of action.

The wind picked up slightly, and there was a whisper of sound from the right. Haven felt his body clench in expectation of an attack, and it hit him hard. Not physically, though, mentally. There was a piercing pain to his right temple, and he went down to one knee. *Ambush!* he screamed through the team's connection.

There was movement all around him, but he could only distantly feel it through the pain in his mind. This was worse than anything he'd ever felt before, and he knew it was an enhanced mercenary he'd never met. It was not an energy signature he recognized, and neither was the ability. Haven struggled to rebuild his mental shields, but they'd been shattered by the vicious attack. Gritting his teeth, he opened his eyes, searching for his attacker. He only had a direction, and that was to the right. He lunged that way. If he couldn't fight his attacker mentally, he needed to take him out physically.

The attacker seemed surprised by his move, because the drilling pain wavered. Then it steadied, and Haven was taken to his knees again, clutching his head.

It sounded like there was more fighting behind him, but he couldn't afford to let his attention waver. He needed to find this man and take him out. In desperation, he pulled his weapon. If he used it, there would be no more surprise. If he didn't use it, his mind might be wrecked forever.

Haven lifted his weapon, paused, shifted, and fired three shots, in the direction he thought the attack was coming from. The drilling pain stopped, and he moved forward. Gunfire erupted from a tree about ten feet ahead, and he jumped to the side, returning fire. He heard a man cry out, and he moved forward faster. He found a masked mercenary laying on the ground. The man lifted his hand, and Haven knew he was about to be attacked again. He put a bullet in the man's forehead.

Turning, he ran for the others. They were all involved in fights. Copper was drilling on a man at least half a head taller than himself, but his punches were having little effect. Dex was fighting with someone out front, but he couldn't tell who. And Donna... He scanned the area, wondering where she'd gone. He opened his senses, but his mind screamed with pain. Whatever that merc had done, there were going to be lasting effects.

There was a surge of power down at the cabin, and Haven ran for it. That had to be Donna. Then there was a scream that terrified him. It was abruptly cut off, and he prayed everyone was all right.

THE FIRST MAN that attacked her was a child. Without even being near him, Donna threw a bolt of power through the unfamiliar brain, burning him out. He would never hurt anyone ever again. The second man that attacked in concert with the first surprised her. He snuck up behind her and wrapped her in his arms, hoisting her off her feet. He started to drag her toward the cabin, but Donna struggled. Her mind sought his, but there was an impenetrable wall surrounding his psyche. She fought him both physically and mentally, but neither worked. In desperation, she hammered her heels into his kneecaps, and he paused. His grip loosened just a tiny bit, just enough that she could get a hand to the knife strapped to her chest. She pulled it, twisted her hand, and shoved it into his body. There was resistance at first, like it was going through a couple of layers of cloth, then it slid in. She wasn't even sure what she was stabbing, exactly, but it didn't matter. She worked the knife back and forth until he released her, then, spinning on her knees, she turned and stabbed at him several times, going for center mass and lower, toward the groin where bullet-proof vests didn't cover. She felt blood spray her face, but she didn't care, she kept swinging and stabbing.

A fist struck her in the side of the head, blindsiding her, and she cried out. She hadn't seen the third man coming through the dark of the night. Grabbing her sidearm, she aimed at the first shadow looming over her and fired three quick shots, then emptied her mag into the one on the ground. The body jerked above her, and finally collapsed. Donna scrambled away, her ears ringing. Even as she pushed to her feet, she reached for her second mag, releasing the first and slamming the second home. She dropped the slide and scanned the area.

The gun didn't do her any good as she was tackled from the side. Her face scraped along the hard ground, and the weight on her back was massive. It felt like her bones creaked, threatening to break. Her hands were folded beneath her, but there was no way she was releasing her weapon.

"Hold her down," someone growled, and the weight on her back seemed to grow heavier. Then she felt something that almost made her piss her pants. The other man was trying to wrap a collar around her neck.

*Haven!* she screamed, panic almost paralyzing her.

No, she refused to be collared again! She fought like a wildcat, wriggling beneath the giant holding her down, and tried to focus her mind. The second man was slimy. She couldn't get a grip on him. And she couldn't burrow inside. The panic was about to overwhelm her, but she fought like she'd never fought before, and she felt the tiniest crack in the man's shields. Using her power like a jackhammer, she pounded into him again and again. Then she burrowed her metaphorical fingers inside, ripping it open. The man cried out, but he squeezed her neck all the harder.

Then the man disappeared, his hands away from her neck. Donna wasn't sure what had happened, but she was thankful. The man holding her down jerked, then jerked again. The third time, he toppled away from her. Donna looked up, and in the weak light from the moon, she saw a hulking shape with iron tipped fingers dripping with blood. Zed? His beady eyes blinked at her, then he turned and lumbered toward another fight.

Then Haven was there, gripping her arms and lifting her to her feet. *Are you okay?*

She nodded, afraid to say anything because she might cry. But there was no time for that. *We need to find Lilly.*

Haven lurched into a jog, but he seemed off. *Are you okay?* she asked him.

*I'm fine*, he said, and she could hear the growl in his mental voice.

Donna sent some energy through him, and found his shattered shields. Oh, Haven... Quickly, she began to repair what she could, but she only had seconds as they ran toward the cabin. Before they could reach it, a wall of air hit them, knocking them backwards off their feet. Dex had been moving in from the side, and he got knocked back as well.

Donna reached for the consciousness of the man

standing on the porch. She recognized Vincent immediately, from the snapshots in Stafford's mind. This was the man responsible for running them down, hurting them, and now trying to steal her daughter. With a slight smile, Donna stood up. "Hello, Dante Vincent," she said.

Vincent cocked his head at her. "Hello, Ms. Frame. It's a pleasure to finally meet you. Call me Vincent, please." He glanced out into the night, and she hoped he was tallying up the injuries to his team.

Donna felt Copper take a position outside the circle of light from the cabin. He was worse for wear, but his nerves were steady as he sighted through his scope toward Vincent.

Donna heard the double click on the mic, which was their indicator to Krammer that they needed backup. She was surprised Haven had waited this long to signal him. Or maybe he'd signaled before and she just hadn't heard.

Vincent cocked his head as he looked at their group. "My intel was outdated. You people were a good challenge."

Haven glanced at the bodies beyond. "Yours weren't."

Donna wanted to laugh at the cockiness of the statement. And she wanted to laugh even more when Vincent's jaw hardened.

"All joking aside, things will go easier on everyone if you surrender to me, Ms. Frame."

Donna choked out a laugh. "You are completely out of your head. There's no way I'm allowing you to collar me again."

Vincent waved a hand, and Roger materialized, standing in front of the open cabin door. He held Lilly, one arm tight around her neck. A gun glinted in his other hand, and the muzzle was buried in her daughter's side. Lilly's hands were bound behind her back, and there were tears in her eyes.

She made a noise, though she was gagged, and Donna knew she'd just said 'Mom'.

"Hey, baby," Donna murmured. She wanted to rush the porch and fold her daughter into her arms, but she couldn't. If that gun went off, it would tear through her daughter's insides, wreaking havoc.

"We'll let your daughter go," Vincent said softly, his voice wrapping around her. "You just have to come with us and help us out with the new subjects."

The words weren't crazy. Maybe they would let Lilly go if she went with them. As a mother, it was her job to sacrifice her life for her daughter's. Right?

"We don't want unnecessary bloodshed," Vincent continued, his voice low and sonorous. "There's been too much already. We just need your help."

One of her feet moved forward.

*Donna! There's something about his voice that's wrong.*

She jerked at the sound of Haven's mental yell, and went still. Had she just been about to walk up to Vincent and volunteer to go with him? She blinked, realizing she'd lost a few seconds of time. That must be his ability, the power of persuasion. Now that she knew, she could feel the tendrils of energy wrapping around her. How could she use that knowledge to her own benefit? If she could get close enough to touch him...

*Trust me*, she said, sending a super-focused thought to Haven.

Even as she wove a protective shield around the team, she tilted her head like she was listening to Vincent. She took a reluctant step forward. He was rambling on about making the country a serious super-power, with soldiers no one could stand against, and his energy continued to tug at her. Now that she saw the manipulation, she couldn't un-see it. She took another step.

Three more steps and she would be within reach. He

would be as well, though. So far, he hadn't made any defensive move. Did he honestly believed she was under his spell?

"Donna," Haven said, and she turned her head slightly. There were men coming out of the darkness, men she didn't recognize. She couldn't afford the energy to scan them right now. It was all she could do to protect the herself and the men from Vincent's siren song. She looked at Lilly. The girl didn't seem to be any worse for the wear. She still wore the same clothes she'd been taken in, but she'd been fed and cared for.

Roger eyed her warily. "Don't trust her, Vincent."

"Are you okay, Lilly?"

Her daughter nodded, her dark hair mussed around her face. She jerked her head toward Roger, and Donna grinned.

"Don't worry, he's a dead man walking," Donna said. She looked directly at Dante Vincent. "I will go with you willingly, if you give me Roger McCullough."

There was a harsh burst of laughter from McCullough, but she stared hard at Vincent's pale eyes. One side of his crooked mouth tipped up in a grin.

"Oh, Ms. Frame, I think you might be a dangerous woman." He eyed her, considering, but he didn't even spare McCullough a glance. "It would solve several issues," he murmured.

"You can't be serious," McCullough said, facing Vincent more fully. "We just did a deal. I'm an asset."

Vincent shrugged. "Your job was to get me in front of Ms. Frame, and you've done that. Our business is concluded. Yes, Ms. Frame, you can have him."

That was when the shit hit the fan.

# 17

Lilly felt the shroud start to roll over them again, and she knew Roger was going to try to get away. With a hard lunge, she jerked away from him, then immediately spun with the knife in her hand. Thoughts of the classes Haven had made them take rolling through her brain. She'd been waiting years to do this, and she wasn't going to let Roger go. Slashing out, she caught him in the chest. He wasn't dressed like the rest of the men. It wasn't a heavy cut, but it was enough to slice through his shirt, shocking him. Unfortunately, he rallied quickly, and slammed a hand to her chest to knock her back. Lilly fell on her ass behind Vincent, but she still had the knife clutched in her hand.

Roger bolted across the deck and jumped off the edge, and in that split second, she decided to let him go. She thought she saw Dex take off after him, limping hard. Vincent appeared to be locked into some kind of silent duel with her mother. Without hesitation, Lilly reached out and slammed the knife down into the top of Vincent's black boot. The knife sank deep, and he yelled out, staggering, his concentration broken.

That was all her mother and Haven needed to overwhelm him. Haven landed punch after punch, but Vincent fought like a beast. Until her mother slapped a hand upon his forehead. He went still, his eyes going unfocused before they drifted shut.

A shot rang out behind them, then another and another, and Lilly went flat to the floor of the porch. When there were no more shots, she glanced around, but she couldn't tell where the shots had come from.

Her mother was watching her from less than a foot away, and Lilly lunged into her arms, ripping the nasty gag from her mouth. She tried to be strong, but the tears came, and they just wouldn't stop. Her mother held her tight, though Lilly could feel her looking around, making sure they were out of danger.

Copper came out of the darkness, limping hard, and he propped his AR across his arms, at the low-ready. "The area appears clear. As soon as you took Vincent down, his backup team disappeared. They just faded into the night. I think I took out a couple of them, but they were more concerned with bugging out than anything."

Haven was rolling Vincent over and strapping his hands with a thick velcro strap, then connecting his ankles to it. Lilly would have laughed, but she was still crying. She pulled away and looked at her mother, but she was crying too. Maybe it was okay for them to take a minute together.

DONNA FELT Haven hovering behind her. Reaching back a hand, she pulled him into their hug. His big arms wrapped around them, and she was so thankful that things had turned out the way they needed to.

"Did anyone get McCullough?" she murmured.

Lilly pulled back, wiping her face and sniffing away her tears. "Dex took off after him, when he ran."

"I was so proud of you, when you struck out at him," Donna said, beaming at her daughter. "Where did you get the knife?"

Lilly snorted. "From his pocket. And I cut myself free in the bathroom, where they were keeping me."

Laughing, she pressed a kiss to her resilient child's forehead. "Good job, baby."

"I'd better go check on Dex," Haven murmured, frowning into the night.

Donna watched him limp in the direction McCullough had escaped. The team was a little worse for wear, but they would be okay. The most important thing was, they'd gotten Lilly back.

Eventually, Haven and Dex returned, and they were hauling a bleeding Roger McCullough between them. Donna grinned, and immediately moved to knock him out. Her energy was so depleted, but she had enough to do that. They let Roger fall where he stood, then checked his restraints. Eventually, they would check his wounds, but that was after they'd cared for their own.

"Where is our backup?" Dex growled. "I heard you click at least three times."

Haven shook his head, worry running through him. "Not sure. We had an open line through most of the fight, but at some point we got disconnected."

Haven pulled his cell phone from one of the vest's pockets and dialed. Dial tone. He backed out of that screen and went to another number. Dr. Cole answered on the first ring. "Haven?"

"Yeah, we're good. Lilly is safe. We have a few injuries, but we'll recover. Are you in contact with the Dog Pound?"

"Yes," she said, her voice low, and he didn't like her intonation.

"What?" he demanded.

Dr. Cole choked out a sob. "The building was attacked. Five men were killed, and baby Fallon was almost taken."

Haven blinked, not sure he'd heard her right. He looked at Donna, and he knew she sensed something was wrong. "Okay. We have to hike out of here, and we'll get on the chopper. We'll pick you and Jibari up, and head back to Virginia."

"Jibari has already left to meet you. I couldn't stop him. He'll find you. Don't worry about me. I have the Delta team with me, and Kevin Rose is on his way. I'll get a ride back with him."

"Roger that," Haven said, and he hung up. Then he looked at his team. "The Pound was attacked. They killed several men, not sure who yet, and tried to take the baby. We need to get home."

That got everybody moving. Within minutes they were loading McCullough and Vincent into the old car McCullough had been driving, and they were speeding for their cabin and the chopper. The pilot was already cycling the machine up when they pulled in, and they loaded everyone on. Jibari appeared out of the darkness, his white smile broad in his dark face. He took the enthusiastic back claps, and settled into the seat beside them.

Haven's head throbbed, but he nodded and talked and related what had happened while their 4th was in the hospital. Jibari looked amazingly fresh. Haven glanced at Donna. She hadn't let Lilly go since they'd found her. Actually, he didn't think either one of them would be letting go of the other in the near future.

They flew through the night and into the morning. Haven managed to grab a few minutes of sleep, but he didn't feel rested when he woke. His head throbbed, and he fought nausea as the helicopter banked around the city. He had no idea what they were walking into.

DONNA HELD her daughter all the way home, through the helicopter ride, the SUV ride. She kept contact with her at all times, and worried that they were going to be ambushed on the way back to the Elton Building. Just in case, she kept her weapons on, just like the rest of the team, and made sure that Lilly still had that damn knife that had been so handy for her.

A team from the CIA had met them at the airport, and they were now sandwiched between their vehicles. Donna didn't feel like they were much safer. And as she pulled up to the Elton building and saw all the extra personnel, she still didn't feel especially safe.

They pulled down into the shadowed cave of the parking garage. When she stepped out of the SUV, she wasn't prepared for the destruction that was visible. It had been an all-out attack. One of the massive metal overhead security gates were down, pushed to the side in a crumpled mess. The SUV they got out of had bullet-holes in the side, as did most of the vehicles down here. The security guards had been killed here, she knew.

They headed into the building through three separate security entry points, and as soon as they made it through, Haven made a beeline straight for Wulfe. They were ushered into a conference room, and given bottles of water.

"So, what do we know?" Haven said, squinting and the glare from the overhead light.

"It seemed like a rushed attack. Like they'd been told we were down on manpower, and they just thought they were going to waltz in and have their way with us." Wulfe shrugged, and Donna realized how tired he was. "The men upstairs rallied. We even had some getting out of their hospital beds to fight, but the assault team never made it through the parking garage. The baby was safe at all times. I had been advised by a certain team leader that I needed to bulk up our security, so I'd called Holtman. He send me a detachment from the Marine Corp Security group, attached to the US Embassy."

Haven smiled slightly, glad that Wulfe had listened to him.

"Angela must be terrified," Donna murmured.

Wulfe tipped his head at her. "She's not happy, by any means. None of us are. But we're locked down and we have support from the CIA and the Deltas. Lilly," he said, turning to her, "I'm very glad that you made it home safely."

Lilly's cheeks turned pink at the attention, and Donna could feel her embarrassment. The girl hadn't had a shower in almost three days, and she was ready to go upstairs and get cleaned up. "Thank you, sir," she murmured. Then she rallied, straightening in her chair. "Is Tini okay?"

Wulfe stared at her for a long moment, then nodded. "They were escorted home the same day after being 'mugged'," he said pointedly, and Lilly nodded, getting the message. "We explained that you would have to reschedule when you'd received proper permission for them to be here."

Her cheeks flamed an even deeper color. "Yes, sir. I'm sorry," she said, looking up at him and glancing at the team around her. "I just got so excited about seeing my friend that security took a back seat. I'll never do anything like this again."

Sighing, Wulfe shrugged. "We all make mistakes. Yours was deadly, though. And it could have been deadlier."

Nodding, she sank back into her chair, tears rolling slowly down her cheeks.

Donna knew her daughter needed the tough love, but it was hard not to reach out to her.

"So far, the media has no idea this kidnapping happened," Wulfe continued. "We've managed to keep it quiet. We are looking at options to get the baby out of the city, and moving you two is not off the table either. I suggest you go upstairs, get cleaned up and relax for a while till we get the mess cleaned up down here. We'll do a full debrief in the morning, after you've had a chance to rest."

They didn't need to be told twice. Standing up, Donna urged Lilly out of the room ahead of her, Haven and the team bringing up the rear. The thought of leaving the facility sent a shudder of fear through her. Lilly was still crying, so Donna didn't know if she'd heard that last bit or not. She glanced back at Haven.

*Don't borrow trouble,* he thought at her. *Wulfe is in crises mode right now, and he's up to his asshole in alligators demanding answers. Give him time to settle down and get his head on straight again.*

Yeah, maybe he was right. It wouldn't do to borrow trouble.

The entire team piled onto the elevator and escorted Donna and Lilly to their door. A security team was already up there, standing guard. Haven waved his own team off duty, then escorted them inside. As soon as the door closed, Lilly turned into her mother's arms, sobbing.

"I never meant to get anyone killed, Mom," she gasped, and Donna's heart broke for her daughter. Yes, she'd been a part of the mess for years, but this was the first time she'd misstepped.

"Security is in place for a reason. This is the world we live in, Lilly-bean. We have to be careful because if we're not, people we care about will be harmed. The senator's men are always looking for weaknesses, and you gave them that opening this time."

Lilly lifted her tear-streaked face, looking at Haven. "I'm sorry Jibari got hurt, and I'm sorry you're hurt. I was selfish, and I didn't even realize how much."

Haven gave her a lopsided smile. "You're okay, kid. This is a lesson learned. For all of us."

She nodded emphatically, then swiped the tears from her cheeks. She took a deep breath, and straightened her shoulders. "I'm going to go clean up, and I think I might sleep. In the morning, I have my own, private apology tour to go on. I need to know the men who died." Her eyes started to tear up again, but she forced them back and turned for her mother. "I love you, Mom," she said, wrapping her arms tight around Donna's neck.

"I love you too, baby," Donna murmured, returning the bone-cracking hug. "Go take a nice hot shower. You might have to wash your hair a couple of times," she said, waving a hand beneath her nose as Lilly pulled away.

Lilly rolled her eyes. "Right..."

They watched her daughter leave, and Donna knew that the innocence she'd once had was gone. She was just glad that Lilly hadn't been hurt more.

"She'll be fine," Haven murmured.

Donna turned to him. He sat in the padded chair across from the couch, looking worn out. There were circles beneath his eyes, and lines of tension around his mouth. He held his body like he was battling a migraine.

"I know," she said softly. Then she shifted to the end of the couch. "Come over here," she told him.

Looking concerned, Haven pushed to his feet and circled the table between them. Then he sat beside her. "What do you need?"

Donna's heart melted at his obvious concern for her. She

shook her head, patting her thigh. "I want you to lay down, and put your head right here. I can see the pain you're in, and we need to fix it."

"I'm fine," Haven argued. "I just need rest."

"Stop arguing," she ordered. "And turn around."

Haven looked at her thighs, and Donna worried that maybe she should have cleaned up first. She still had dirt and detritus on her from fighting outside the cabin. He was looking at her lap, though, like it was the softest bed he'd ever seen. After a slight hesitation, he turned on the cushion, and laid down, resting his head on her thigh. "This isn't what I came in here for," he said, voice soft, and she smiled slightly.

"I know that."

As soon as she rested her hands on his his head, she felt the pain he was in. Oh, lord, it was excruciating. His shields were rubble, and the merest touch against his mind made him wince. Thinking cooling thoughts, she eased a balm over the cuts the enemy merc had left. The guy had obliterated their months of work.

"You killed this guy, right?"

It took him a minute to answer. "I did," he whispered.

"Good, because this is a terrible ability."

For several long minutes, she did what she could to ease the pain in his mind. It was hard, though. She was tired as well, and once, she accidentally scraped against a raw spot when she didn't control her own power. Haven jerked, and when she looked down, it broke her heart to see tears leak from the corners of his eyes and down to her thighs. "It's okay," he rasped. "Keep going."

Centering, she tightened the focus of her healing, rebuilding his shield block by block. By the time she was done, almost half an hour had passed by, and they were both exhausted.

Donna rested her hands on his head, stroking his short

hair softly. He'd long ago fallen asleep, and he barely opened his eyes as she slipped out from beneath him. Pulling a soft blanket from the back of the couch, she covered him with it and turned off the lights as she headed to her own bedroom. It took the rest of her energy to take a quick shower, then crawl into her own bed.

## 18

The aftermath was stark. Haven and his team surveyed the damage to the interior of the building the next morning, walking through the destruction they could see.

The parking garage needed a lot of work. The damaged vehicles were parked on one side, waiting for repair or destruction. One of the SUVs wouldn't start, and they'd found bullet holes through the block. Their attackers had been using heavy duty weapons. There were holes in the concrete supports of the building. A structural engineer would have to come in to check that the building wasn't going to fall down around them.

"How did they get this far in, though? And did they drive out the same way?"

They went up to Krammer's office, looking for answers. He already had the footage keyed up. Two dark SUVs pulled up to the salley-port gate, the fenced area between two checkpoints. Someone leaned out, keyed in the code for the outer gate, then pulled through. They were between the fences when they started the attack on the second, guarded gate.

"How did they get through that?" Jibari asked, pointing at the screen. "They had the exterior code."

"Which changes every day," Haven murmured, and they all looked at one another.

At one time, he'd thought of the daily changing code as a pain in the ass. The fact that they'd used it yesterday told them they either had a mole in the group, or a worm in the system.

Haven was more apt to believe they had a mole. And he knew who was at the top of his list. He would have to talk to Wulfe or Aiden about investigating him, though.

They watched the footage, and refused to flinch as some of their own men were gunned down. They fought hard, and Haven was gratified to see several of the aggressors go down as well. After about a minute of heavy gunfire, the Marine detachment arrived as backup, and the invading crew evacuated. Total elapsed time, about three minutes.

"Krammer, do up a file of faces and backgrounds. As many as you can see."

"Already working on it," he said, keyboard clacking. "I should have a fairly complete file by this evening."

Haven looked at Dex and the others. "You guys keep on him. Let me know if you spot anything big. I need to go talk to Lilly."

Immediately, the men began razzing him, but he waved them off. "Be good, assholes. Go do something constructive."

HAVEN HEADED up to the greenhouse, looking for his target. He knew he'd found her because he found the extra guards he'd assigned her. They gave him a nod, and pointed in a direction. Haven wove through the plants, and found Lilly sitting at one of the bistro tables, her computer open. She was reading on a screen, scrolling occasionally, but she looked up when he stopped beside her.

"Mind if I sit down," he asked.

She waved him to the opposite chair. "Nope. What's up?"

"Nothing in particular. I kind of just wanted to check on you."

Lilly tilted her head, frowning slightly. "I'm fine. You checked on us the other night, too. I really am doing okay."

She looked away and she started to blink a lot, like she was fighting tears, but Haven didn't point that out. "Okay. I just wanted to make sure. I know the past couple of days haven't been a walk in the park, so..."

She shrugged, running a finger over the edge of her computer. "It's okay. I did what I needed to do to. Mom said there's a chance we could be moved out of here? But where would be more secure than the Elton building?"

Haven shifted in the chair, frowning. "Nothing has been decided about that. Right now it is just about the most secure place you can be. I watched the tapes of the attack, and our men repelled them easily. Yes, we had casualties, but they had more. They just gathered up their injured and dead and took them with them when they left."

She nodded, absorbing the information. "If I have any kind of say in the matter, I don't want to go anywhere."

Nodding, Haven gave her a reassuring smile. "I'll be sure Wulfe knows that." He shifted in his chair, looking out through the greenhouse. "So, I have another reason for searching you out."

Lilly gave him a lopsided smile, one dark eyebrow raised. Haven had a feeling she knew what he wanted to ask her, but she was going to make him actually say it. Her shields were locked down tight, so he had no idea what she was thinking. "I, uh, I like your mom. A lot. And I'd like to ask her to dinner, if you wouldn't mind."

She stared at him for several long seconds, almost long enough to make him squirm, and Haven let his smile spread. This kid needed to be an interrogator in a few years.

"I'm fine with it," she said eventually, "but you have to think about the ramifications if you develop a relationship. And then what if you break up? That would make things really awkward."

"Just a minute," he said, laughing, as he held up a hand. "You're kind of jumping the gun a little bit. I just want to ask her to dinner. I don't think your mom is ready for more than that anyway."

Lilly leaned back in her chair, her blue eyes glinting with humor. "I know. I'm actually surprised you haven't asked her before now. I think you guys are cute together and I absolutely think you should invite her to dinner. Better yet, set up the dinner and surprise her with it."

Frowning, he thought about that. "Do you think she would like that?"

Lilly nodded, leaning forward on her elbows. "You could do it up here. Nic can make you something nice. Just tell her you want to talk about something and she would be more than happy to come up and see you. It would be a nice surprise."

Yeah, maybe it would.

## 19

Four days later, Haven felt like he was going to go crazy. He took a deep breath and ran his hand over his shirt collar, and the buttons marching down his chest, as he stood at the elevator landing on the roof. It had been forever since he'd worn anything other than some kind of military uniform, and he squirmed. Noah had sworn that this was proper dating attire, though, and he would have to take him at his word.

Noah taking him shopping yesterday had been a little surreal. They lived such a cloistered, structured life. Yet, when they went out into public, they were reminded how oblivious people were to the danger around them. Ninety-nine percent of them were soft targets, cannon fodder, just waiting for the next emergency they could blast on social media. And none of them had any kind of shields, either physical or mental. They just broadcast what was in their brain. It was tiring going out and blocking all that out.

He'd found what he'd wanted, though, and Noah had guided him toward an outfit.

Now he was rethinking it. He doubted Donna would care

what he wore, and he didn't want to make her feel uncomfortable that she hadn't changed into something date worthy. He glanced at his watch, wondering if he had time to run downstairs and change into jeans or something. Even as he thought it, he heard the elevator ping. She was already on her way up. Hell.

He just had to roll with it, and hope it was okay.

The elevator door pinged when it arrived to the floor, and he held his breath as the doors slid apart.

Donna stepped off the car and stopped when she saw him, her hands clasped tight in front of her as her gaze caught his. Haven was floored. She looked stunning. Her dark hair was down, and curled slightly, hanging over one shoulder. It looked soft and appealing, and he wanted to run his hands through it. She'd also put makeup on. Her eyes looked bigger and darker, and there was a deep pink shade on her lips. He'd expected her to be in jeans and a sweatshirt, what she normally wore, but instead she wore a pale green colored shirt and tan khakis, with a light sweater.

"How did you know?" he said softly, looking her up and down.

Her face turned quizzical. "I'm not sure exactly. Something told me I needed to clean up a little." A smile spread her mouth and she lifted her brows. "Did I do okay?"

Haven cursed himself for not telling her first thing how beautiful she was to him. "Yes, you look amazing." He stepped forward, taking her hands in his. "I was struck dumb when you stepped off."

Her smile widened, and she glanced down. "I'm really glad I listened to my instincts, then. You look... incredible, as well."

Haven thought he could blush at the way she looked at him, but he grinned. He wore a pale olive green button down, and khakis very similar to her own. "Thank you. Noah took me shopping."

Donna laughed, nodding her head. "We'll have to tell him he did good."

They stood there for a minute, just kind of looking at each other, before they laughed. Haven held out a hand. "Would you join me?"

Donna let him lead her deeper into the greenhouse. In the midst of some of the prettiest, biggest blooms, he'd set up a square table with a black cloth. Nic had helped him out with that, smiling as she set the table for them, explained what she'd left under the silver cloches and the order they were to be served in. The woman had seemed ecstatic to be helping him with his date, and Haven made sure to tell her how much he appreciated what she'd done. And just a few minutes ago, the main lights had dimmed, and tiny little fairy lights had come to life, strung around their little space. He wasn't sure if Nic had done it or someone else, but he would figure it out and thank them.

Donna looked at the set-up, and her eyes turned a little glossy in the gentle light. "You did this for me?"

Haven crossed to one of the chairs and held it out for her to be seated. "Of course. I told you we were going to go on a date once all this mess was settled, and it's been almost a week. I thought that was enough time."

He reached for the bottle of moscato chilling in a bucket. He popped the cork and poured her a glass, setting it in front of her. He would have preferred beer, but Nic had suggested that this would be good with the dinner she'd created. Haven took a sip when he sat down, and he was surprised at how mellow it was. Yeah, beer was good, but this was a nice change.

Donna seemed to think so too. She smiled as she took a couple of little sips. "I hardly ever let myself drink."

Haven nodded, understanding. With their mental abilities, they needed to keep their wits about them at all times. "I don't feel like this is going to be too much," he murmured. "Especially if we eat. I hope you're hungry?"

Nodding, she sat up in her chair, her hands in her lap, and watched as he set the appetizer in front of her, her eyes alight with happiness. Haven had to pause, because she absolutely took his breath away. Donna seemed to be caught in the moment as well, because she reached a hand up, obviously wanting him to bend down. Their mouths met in the most instinctual, natural way, and Haven knew that he was going to be ruined for anyone else. Very deliberately, he let his shields fall so that she could feel everything he was experiencing. Donna cupped his head in her hands, and their mouths danced. They licked and kissed and nibbled, and when he finally let her go, they were both breathless.

"You dropped your shields," she murmured, looking deep into his kind eyes.

"I wanted you to feel how you affect me," he said simply. "But there are no obligations. I want to make that very clear. This is a dinner. I want to know you, Donna Frame. Not just what you project. And we'll take as much time as you need to get comfortable with me."

She nodded, rocked by his honesty, and wanted to tell him that she was already comfortable with him, but she was afraid to voice the words. Maybe after a little more moscato.

Donna wanted to cry several times throughout the night, but she fought to stay in control.

Haven had created a magical experience for her. Yes, they were required to stay in a single building right now, but she didn't feel deprived as he fed her a sublime dinner. Nicolette had outdone herself tonight, and Donna would have to tell her how amazing the food had been. They talked about mundane things, like what kind of child she'd been, and what cartoons she'd watched after school, what kind of student she'd been. They laughed and giggled through their memories, staying away from anything dark, and Donna couldn't remember having a better time in the past five years.

After dinner, he helped her up from the chair and guided her down the path, to a more open part of the greenhouse. Here, an incredibly stuffed couch had been brought up from somewhere, facing one of the walls. As she watched, a screen rolled down from the ceiling, and credits started playing for a popular movie.

Donna laughed, and dropped down to the cushions of the couch. "The Wizard of Oz? Really?"

"Hey, it's a classic," Haven said, settling into the corner of the couch. He reached down beside him and pressed a button, and the feet folded out. He opened his arm to her, and Donna was helpless to refuse. She settled in against his warm body, and didn't argue when he pulled a blanket from the floor to cover them with. Yes, she'd watched movies with her daughter in a similar way, but this was a very different experience. The entire time he held her, she was cognizant of him as a man.

He didn't expect anything of her, though. She read that very clearly in him. He wanted to give her a magical experience, and maybe get a kiss at the end of the night. That was as far as his thoughts ranged, and Donna found herself a little put out that he didn't want more from her. It was so messed up, because he was being a perfect gentleman.

And she kind of wanted him not to be.

She looked at the movie playing on the screen. The Wizard of Oz was about as sexless as you could get in a movie. Had he chosen it specifically for that reason? The thought badgered at her. When she'd come out of the shower a week ago, she'd felt the instant want he'd had for her.

Shields down, his need had poured into her, and it had taken her by surprise. But she wanted to feel it again.

Her breathing picked up as the credits began to roll, and she wondered if she had the courage to do what she'd done before.

"I want you to know how much I've enjoyed tonight," he told her, his voice rumbling beneath her ear.

"I have, too," she whispered, pushing away to sit up a little. It put them nearly eye to eye, and she took the initiative, leaning forward to kiss him.

Haven groaned, cupping her head as she leaned into him, and because his shields were down, she could feel the heady rush of arousal that swirled down through his body. It made her gasp, her body responding just as strongly. It took Donna by surprise, the need, because it had been so long. But she suddenly craved his touch. To the very fiber of her being, she knew that Haven would not hurt her in any way. She could literally see in his mind how worried he was for her, and his determination not to move too fast. And that gave her the freedom to open up to him as she'd never done before with another man.

When she began to unbutton her shirt, his eyes widened, and he immediately began to shake his head. "Donna, that's not necessary. I didn't set this up for that."

She continued to unbutton the shirt, and when she reached the end, she shrugged it from her shoulders, her gaze on his.

"We're not rushing," he said firmly, holding her gaze. "I want this to be a long-term relationship, not just a quick grind on a couch."

Donna smiled slightly, reaching behind her back for the clasp of her bra. "Did you ever play around with a girl on a couch?" she teased.

His ears turned a little pink. "There may have been one or two."

He had incredible determination, but as soon as she shrugged the bra away, his gaze dropped, and his face went slack with need. But he didn't move, and his mouth tightened. His control was like iron. She could feel the determination in him not to move, and it made her that much more determined to make him respond. They were in a battle of wills she never expected to be in, and she was determined to win tonight.

Reaching out, she lifted one of his hands to cup her breast. "We're not rushing, Haven. I've wanted you for a very long time, but I was scared. Obviously, for many different reasons. But maybe," she hesitated, "maybe if you let me take the lead, we can see where we end up."

His eyes flared with heat, and he gave her a single nod. "I swear to you, I will not move unless you tell me to, Donna. I want this to be your time. You do what you need to do, and we'll stop whenever you need to. I love you."

She'd felt the words floating in his mind, but hearing them spoken aloud shook her to her core. She gasped out a sob, which totally wasn't the mood she was going for, but she couldn't help it, and she shook her head. "I don't understand. How can you love me? I've done terrible things."

Haven's eyes narrowed with laughter. "Are you serious? You are, literally, the strongest woman I know. And you have an incredible love inside you. But you had to hide that love for a while." He pulled at her hair a little, winding it through his fingers. "You fought what happened to you, and I've seen the love you have for your daughter, and for your patients, and even the men that you've help recover that won't give you the time of day yet."

She snorted, and wiped the tears away, taking his words into her heart.

"It's why you got into nursing in the first place, your incredible love of people." He stroked a finger down her cheek. "Like I said, I love you, and I can see what you can't. I've seen how much you've changed in the past year, and I know how scared you are to open your heart. But I'm willing to wait to see you bloom."

Heaving a deep breath, she leaned in to kiss him again. No one had ever offered their unconditional support like that, and it made her feel like she could do anything. Taking her courage in hand, she twisted to straddle his hips.

Haven immediately closed his eyes, and she thought she heard him desperately counting, but she could feel how much he wanted her. There was a rigid length running straight up his belly, hidden by the fabric of his pants. It made her grin, and she rocked forward a little, making them both gasp. "Open your eyes, Haven."

He did as she told him to do, but he kept his hands to the side. And he maintained eye contact with her. Donna leaned down, pressing kisses along the length of his face. And she began to unbutton his shirt. "I want you to look at me, Haven, and I want you to touch me. I want you to show me your need."

He made an inarticulate sound in his throat. "If I do that, there's a very good chance you're going to make me come in my pants."

Donna grinned, tugging at his shift tails, nibbling at his lips. "That's a risk we're going to have to take."

Then his hands were on her, running up the length of her back, and Donna quivered inside. Grabbing his wrists, she pulled them forward, making him cup her breasts, as she looked down at him. She'd seen Haven shirtless before, and she'd always been curious about the line of dark hair that went straight down his abs. She ran a finger down it, stopping at his waistband. A bolt of pleasure rolled down through her body, and she wasn't sure if it was his or hers, or maybe a combination of them both.

"Oh, Donna," he whispered. "You are so beautiful." His fingers pinched her nipples, and she cried out. Her hips rocked, needing something, and he shifted beneath her, making the couch go a little flatter, and his hips higher. Then he shifted her pelvis over him, so that she could grind against that rigid length. Donna panted, surprised at how quickly her need had spiked, and she flexed above him.

Haven pressed kisses along her jaw and down, lifting her a little so that he could draw a nipple into his warm mouth, tonguing her hard. Donna cried out, the pleasure more than she'd known in so long. She wiggled her hips against him, the seam of her pants grinding into her clit. She started to move, forward and back, just enough to make her body sing. Then she had to move harder. Haven's pleasure was ramping up as well, his dick swelling with the need to be inside her. His hot mouth moved to her other breast, and a spiral of heat began to tighten in her body. As she moved over top of him, grinding harder and harder, that heat spiked.

Haven gasped, and she felt his orgasm slam through him, and his pleasure triggered her own. With a loud cry, she arched over him, her body clutching and releasing in time with his. The orgasm seemed to go on forever, and it was so incredibly beautiful. She sagged against him, and he wrapped his arms around her, burying his face in her hair. He murmured to her as tears slipped down her cheeks, and stroked her back.

Donna was emotionally wrung out, but proud, too. The worry had been there that they wouldn't even be able to do this much without something crawling out of her psyche to sabotage her happiness. No, they hadn't had sex, but they would, and she knew that it would be more amazing than grinding on the couch. After a minute, she sat up, and looked down at where they joined. There was indeed an impressive dark patch where he'd come in his pants, and she couldn't help but smile.

Haven had a resigned look on his face, but she could feel his satiation, and his pride that she'd been able to overcome this one hurdle. He shrugged, looking smug. "Told you."

Donna laughed, collapsing in his arms.

# EPILOGUE

F our months later...

THEY WERE in the process of moving into the Reserve, and it was more than she ever could have hoped for. When she'd walked up the rope bridge across the rocky gully and into the clearing where their cabin was, she'd been struck speechless. It was beautiful, with broad windows and a long, shallow roof. Inside, there was a beautiful kitchen that may be wasted on her, but she would do her best. She'd gotten proficient in making their own pizzas, at least.

The cabin had an open living area, with a super-comfortable looking couch and matching chair. Donna couldn't even imagine the logistics of getting all this stuff up here. Yes, the decorations were a little spare, but that was alright. They'd all been in the military, so they were used to it.

There were two bedrooms, on opposite ends of the house.

"This one is ours?" she asked, looking at the king sized expanse as Haven led her into the room.

"It is."

This made her so happy, because maybe they were far enough away that Lilly wouldn't comment on any sounds coming from their room. If they were on opposite ends of the building, maybe she wouldn't hear anything. Then Donna walked into the bathroom, and she melted. It was a huge room as well, with a long tiled area big enough to shower ten people. But there was a tub on the opposite side from the shower heads. When had she last taken the time to soak in a tub?

"Oh, my. And we'll have enough water for this?"

Haven nodded. "Fontana has installed instant water heaters. We have the stored rain collection system on the roof, and if that drains we pick up from a secondary source, up the mountain. But it runs completely on solar power."

"This is ours?" she asked faintly.

"If you don't mind living together. I kind of assumed..."

She bumped into his shoulder. "You know I don't."

She wandered back through the rooms, looking at the finishes. Everything was so well done. It was like he'd walked into her mind and just taken notes of what she liked. She opened the door to Lilly's room, and gasped softly.

Her daughter was stretched out on her own queen-sized bed, and she appeared to be sound asleep. They'd just walked into the house minutes ago, but she'd found her zen room. There were orchids on the window sill, and books on the book shelves. There was a TV in one corner, though Haven had already warned her he wasn't sure what the reception would be like. Fontana complained it was hit or miss. There were fuzzy rugs on the floor in Lilly's favorite colors, and she was so thankful that Haven had had the consideration to send Fontana their likes and dislikes. This was perfect for her daughter.

They backed out of the room, closing the door softly behind them. Then Haven took her hand. "This is my favorite part of the cabin."

He led her onto a massive back porch. It stretched from one end of the house to the other, and there was a massive swing hung up on one corner, looking out at the view. Haven pulled her to the hand-hewn railing. Donna looked at the expansive scene in front of her, and could hardly catch her breath. "Haven, this is amazing."

A valley of trees stretched before them, and peak after peak fading into the mist of a beautiful spring landscape. Donna never would have thought that North Carolina would make her fall in love, but it was doing exactly that. Or maybe she'd just developed a pattern.

Turning, she looped her arms around Haven's neck. Immediately, he leaned down to kiss her. "Do you think you'll like it here?" he asked, and she could feel the worry in his heart.

She nodded. "I'm going to love it here, especially if I'm with you."

"I love you, woman. I'll still have a job to do, but know that I will always come home to you. And your burnt pizza."

"You'd better," she warned, laughing. "Because you sweet-talked your way in, made me fall in love with you, and now you're stuck with me. Actually, you're stuck with us."

Haven grinned, his heart and mind wide open to her, and she knew he would love her forever.

ANDRÉ SOLANA SLIPPED into the back of the limousine, and it pulled away from the curb. He settled into the seat, looking at the woman across from him impassively. She was in her mid to late fifties, with iron-gray hair, and didn't look anything like what he knew her to be. She looked like a typical grandmother.

"Is it done?"

"Yes, ma'am. Mr. Pike had a change of heart and signed the papers. I'm sure he's drinking your half-brother's Macallan as we speak. By this time tomorrow he'll be dead, you'll be in charge, and we can do what we need to do in plain sight."

"Oh, I don't know, Mr. Solana. I kind of like being in the shadows. Once I take over, I'm not sure if I'll make it public or not."

"That's completely up to you, ma'am."

She tilted her head at him. "Yes, it is. Let's go see our men, Mr. Solana. We have a lot of catching up and restructuring to do."

THANK you so much for reading the fifth book in the Dogs of War series! If you'd like to stay up to date with my books, please join my newsletter at www.jmmadden.com/newsletter

# ABOUT THE AUTHOR

NY Times and USA Today Bestselling author J.M. Madden writes compelling romances between 'combat modified' military men and the women who love them. J.M. Madden loves any and all good love stories, most particularly her own. She has two beautiful children and a husband who always keeps her on her toes.

J.M. was a Deputy Sheriff in Ohio for nine years, until hubby moved the crew to Kentucky. When not chasing the family around, she's at the computer, reading and writing, perfecting her craft. She occasionally takes breaks to feed her animal horde and is trying to control her office-supply addiction, but both tasks are uphill battles. An eternal optimist, she believes there is a soulmate for everyone, no matter what the situation or physical challenge. She dearly loves to hear from readers! So, drop her a line. She'll respond.

✔www.jmmadden.com

✔My FB Like page- https://www.facebook.com/ JMMadden58

✔Sign up for my Newsletter if you haven't already.

✔Follow me on Instagram- https://www.instagram.com/ jm_madden_58/

✔The Lost and Found Series Discussion Group-https:// www.facebook.com/groups/433871413415527

✔Tiktok- https://www.tiktok.com/@authorjmmadden

OR you can email me at authorjmmadden@gmail.com

# ALSO BY JM MADDEN

If you would like to read about the 'combat modified' veterans of the **Lost and Found Investigative Service**, check out these books:

There are two Lost and Found Spinoff series, the Lowells, a western series, and the Dogs of War, which heads in a paranormal direction.

The Lowells of Honeywell, Texas Box Set

Forget Me Not

Untying his Not

Naughty by Nature

Trying the Knot

The Dogs of War

Genesis

Chaos

Destruction

Retribution

Catalyst

Resurgence

If you love dogs and would like to read about a concierge service helping military personnel out of difficult spots, check out:

Healing Home

Wicked Healing

Healing Hope

**If you would like to read a Navy SEAL book with more mature characters, check out**

**SEAL Hard**

**Flat Line**

**Shadow of the Moon**

**Shadow Games**

Other books by J.M. Madden